ETERNAL ORDER

T.A. Berkeley

ALSO BY T.A. BERKELEY

The Infinity Cure

In an underwater mansion, a wealthy philanthropist holds a summit about a deadly epidemic sweeping through the ancient aquean people. Then, guests start disappearing, and veteran reporter Hiroe Anno joins a young aquean poet and her estranged mentor from a rival news service in an investigation where each new disturbing discovery brings more questions than answers.

Devil's Sanctum

A perfect date becomes a nightmare when a man's new love disappears. And it seems there was a lot he didn't know about his girlfriend. To find her, he embarks on a twisted adventure where his only friend is someone he isn't sure he can trust.

Viral

In this paranormal polyamorous horror thriller, eight teens go to rural West Virginia for what they think will be a carefree vacation. But it turns nightmarish when one starts to read the others' thoughts—including a dark secret about the real reason they left town. Now the group must grapple with a terrifying virus they've brought with them.

READER PRAISE FOR *VIRAL*

"Swift and captivating, T.A. Berkeley's debut novel grabs you from the beginning and doesn't let go as it pulls you along for an eerie and exciting ride!"

"Delicious horror-mystery with plenty of paranoia and psychological mayhem to breeze right through without putting it down."

"Such a fun summer read! … The writing is lean and moves quickly."

"A great, fun thriller (with some saucy bits in there too) that kept me guessing to the end!"

READER PRAISE FOR *DEVIL'S SANCTUM*

"It's fun to just lose myself in a fast-moving thriller. Sex, mystery, action, and one of my favorite things: regular person finds himself suddenly involved in high-stakes international intrigue. He's just a gym teacher who thought he was going to have a chill summer. Oh, Brandon. Not this time."

"Excellent book! I had to force myself to set it down and finish later so I could enjoy it for longer."

For T.N. and B.A., my life partners who make this
life possible

CHAPTER ONE

A huge white moon hangs high in the night sky. It bathes the ground with a milky sheen and illuminates miniscule drops of mist in the air. In its light the leafy vines dripping from trees are a cool grayish green, and its reflection wavers on the surface of a small pond.

A young woman creeps from shadow to shadow, shying away from the generous moonlight. She wears a hoodie made of a soft, flowing material over a skin-tight catsuit, both matte black. The hood's not up, and her dark curly hair practically floats in the air. When she isn't in shadows, it shimmers slightly where it's attracted flecks of moisture.

Anyone on Earth—and several other planets as well—would've stared wide-eyed, her name on their lips, had they seen her. But she's not on Earth, and the only eyes gazing at her are the implacable unblinking orbs of an owl-like creature clinging to the side of a tree with its talons.

It's clear from her body language that she does feel like she's being watched, though it's not the usual knowing, always-posed air of a celebrity who always expects to be spotted. She continually scans the grounds, whispering as if to herself from time to time in a low voice that would have been nearly inaudible to anyone trying to eavesdrop. Her movements are furtive, her shoulders hunched as if to make herself seem smaller.

Something rustles softly behind her, and she jumps with a sharp intake of air like a quiet scream. She swivels sharply and backs away in a defensive crouch, looking wildly in the direction of the sound. The rustle happens again and she sees some long blades of grass near a tree trunk move in a way that suggests a small four-legged creature is creeping away from her. Her exhale of relief turns into a nearly silent giggle.

She walks a little easier, as if the false alarm has released some tension. Down a short slope, she begins to pass buildings, their marble-like exteriors a swirl of green, blue, and white that can be dimly seen in the moonlight. High arches lead to murky interiors, possibly courtyards.

She walks close enough to one building to graze its smooth cool wall with the fingers of her left hand, peering up at it, blinking her eyes rapidly and tapping her right temple with her fingers.

The buildings give way to more greenery, revealing a gentle slope down to a larger pond than the first one she passed. It somehow looks both natural and artfully arranged. The white stones around it are asymmetrical and seemingly placed randomly, but they look perfect, as if there was no better way they could possibly have been positioned. More trees festooned with strings of ivy bend over the pool, leafy tendrils grazing its surface.

The young woman frowns and gets closer, looking intently at the pond, once again blinking and tapping her temple. The water shimmers with something more than moonlight, moves with something other than the breeze stirring the vines.

Another rustling sound behind her. She turns, but less urgently this time, almost smiling as she tries to spot whatever small creature is scampering through the grass.

Instead a human figure slams into her, coming at her from beyond her peripheral vision. The woman hits the ground, the impact knocking the wind out of her lungs and leaving her breathless.

She's stunned for only a second or two before she begins struggling with surprising strength for her slight body. She pushes the attacker off and leaps to her feet, backing away, but the person, face obscured by a balaclava, dives at her again. They grapple on one of the white rocks overhanging the pool, and the woman's feet begin to slip despite the grips on her supple black shoes.

For a moment it seems she might fall into the strange waters. She strains desperately against her assailant and finally throws them back so she can run past them, up the slight slope toward the buildings. She looks behind her and sees them gaining fast, and in her desperation breaks her silence, giving up any vestige of stealth.

"Help me!" she screams, piercing the quiet night and causing several winged creatures to take flight from nearby trees. "Help!" Before she can shout again, the figure tackles her from behind and she falls winded to the ground once again.

This time she's pinned on her stomach under the attacker's full weight, unable to get arms or legs under her or roll to either side, no matter how she struggles. The figure removes a small object from a pocket, turns it on with a quiet beep, and drives it into the helpless woman's side. She screams in pain and lights come on in the two buildings closest to her; a dim, flickering light, as if from candles or gas lanterns.

The assailant looks up, sees no one coming yet, and withdraws the device, only to bring it down into the woman's back several times in quick succession and with brutal force. Her cries soon weaken and her body goes limp.

The occupants of the buildings begin to emerge, running in all directions, searching for the source of the now silenced screams. The attacker leaps up and melts into the darkness.

A young woman, barefoot in two-piece pajamas made of a coarse material, long hair tumbling around her face and shoulders, nearly stumbles over the body of the victim. She looks down in shock, but remains silent, looking around and gesturing wildly. No one notices her gesticulations, so she turns her attention to the fallen figure. She touches the wounds, and then gingerly rolls her over.

As she does, the victim's ashen face comes into view, faintly illuminated by the milky moonlight. The young woman in pajamas cries out and steps back. The sound finally gets the attention of others, who start toward her. She finds words. "It's—it's Crenshaw Connelly! I think she's dead!"

There's a sharp, collective intake of air from multiple people as they gather around, silent.

In the hush, a thin black band around the neck of the woman who had made the discovery lets out a sustained beeping sound. The woman puts her hand to her mouth, eyes wide with another layer of shock and horror.

CHAPTER TWO

Lyndon squeezed his hand around the firearm concealed in his pocket. He moved through dim rooms, walls mottled with unidentifiable stains, furniture askew. His mobile, strapped to his wrist, vibrated quietly. One more person left in the squat, it told him. Nearby.

He spotted a door about two feet tall, a storage cupboard maybe, and moved toward it soundlessly, until the warped floor creaked under his foot.

"Hey," a quiet, strangled voice said from behind the tiny door. "Please, help me."

Lyndon realized he'd been holding his breath in his attempt to stay quiet, and he let it out in relief. Probably just one more junkie hiding from the raid. "Come out," he said, hand still on his firearm. "No one's gonna hurt you."

The door opened a crack. Lyndon saw pale fingers clutching the edge of it. He strained to see a face but it was dark inside the space. "I'm scared."

The voice sounded weak and timid, but the back of Lyndon's neck tingled. He stepped back a foot and tightened his grip on his weapon but kept his own voice soothing. "It's gonna be okay," he said. "I'm here to help. Come on out now."

The door opened fully and a scrawny man in filthy clothing crawled out, his movements tentative, his head lowered.

"Good," Lyndon said. "I'm going to advise you of your rights n—"

The man lifted his head and Lyndon saw his eyes at last, glittering under a tangled mat of hair. He'd encountered enough fink addicts to recognize the expression and drew his firearm as the man suddenly coiled and leapt at him. He shot off a tranquilizer round and dodged as the junkie's body fell forward, unconscious.

"Bates!" His partner Sewell's voice in his ear. "What's going on?"

"All good," Lyndon responded, checking his mobile to make sure it didn't detect anyone else. He hooked his arms under the man's shoulders, grimacing at the smell, and dragged him toward the elevator. "On my way out with the last one."

Another voice broke in. "Good, because you gotta go. Commander wants to see you right away."

Lyndon felt a prickle of unease, even though he couldn't think of anything he'd done wrong. Still, he'd never had Commander Stoughton ask to see him before; he'd only met him once, at the reception following his graduation ceremony.

"Yes sir," he said to the captain. He bit his tongue to keep from asking more. As the new kid on the force he tried hard to exude quiet professionalism. The elevator opened on the dingy lobby and he hauled the still-limp body to the sidewalk where Sewell was waiting.

"Did you hear that—was it on the open channel?" he asked the older man. Sewell nodded, trying to hide his concern, which just made Lyndon more nervous. "You mind seeing the prisoners to lockup so I can go get cleaned up?"

"Sure thing, kid," Sewell said. Lyndon hated being called that, but he was used to it.

The captain spoke up in his ear again. "And put on your dress blues. You're meeting him at Connelly Tower." Lyndon's eyes widened; he and Sewell shared a wordless look of bewilderment.

CHAPTER THREE

A small driverless car, one of many nearly identical ones on the street, whirred to a stop at the curb. Lyndon unfolded himself from his seat and stepped onto the sidewalk. He didn't look back as a harried-looking woman took his place, the car door closed automatically with a click, and the vehicle pulled away.

Dressed in a midnight blue uniform with gold insignia on the breast and shoulders, he walked quickly and purposefully into the hundred-story building in front of him. There was a nearly undetectable nervous energy in his stride, but he was otherwise outwardly calm.

An elevator swept him to his destination on the top floor, and he stepped out into a stunning glass-walled lobby. So different from the squalid building he'd been in just a couple hours ago, it might as well have been a different planet. A man sitting behind a desk—a receptionist, Lyndon thought wonderingly, something he'd only seen in centuries-old classic movies—smiled and greeted him.

"I have an appointment with Connor Connelly," he said, marveling at how matter-of-factly he was able to say it. "I'm Officer Lyndon Bates." The second sentence sounded almost as strange in his ears as the first, even though he'd imagined saying it for years.

The receptionist touched the desk and looked straight ahead as if he were staring at Lyndon's chest, scanning a screen visible only to him.

"Yes," the receptionist confirmed. "He'll send for you shortly, Mr.—sorry, *Officer* Bates."

Lyndon resisted the urge to say he understood, he hardly believed the title himself. Instead he smiled and thanked the man. He walked to the glass wall to look out at the city while he waited. At this height, a couple of four-person carplanes could be seen buzzing around, but the vehicles were still cost-prohibitive and licenses to operate them were challenging to obtain, so there weren't many. All he could mainly see were the tops of lesser skyscrapers dominated by the one he was in.

The minutes passed quickly for Lyndon as he took in the view, and he was soon being ushered down a high-ceilinged hall and into another room.

It was impossible not to be impressed by the palatial chamber he found himself in, but he managed to keep his expression stoic. The imposing furniture included a line of huge, slightly recessed screens that circled the entire room at slightly above eye level, each playing a different program on mute. They gave the room an antique appearance that somehow made it even more impressive.

At the far end of the room, three steps led up to an intricate command center with screens, a keyboard, and a huge chair in the middle. Lyndon couldn't imagine anything that couldn't be handled with a small mobile device or implant, so the setup seemed to have a distinctly theatrical purpose.

Two men sat on a cushioned bench on the platform, drinks in hand. They both looked toward Lyndon as he entered. The young man drew himself up slightly, composing himself, and strode toward them.

"Hi Lyndon, you're right on time," one of the men said in a tone of informal camaraderie. He wore a similar uniform to Lyndon's, differentiated by an abundance of regalia on his coat. He was in his fifties, though with his unlined face and dark hair not containing a single speck of silver, it was hard to tell unless his bearing and uniform were taken into account.

"Thank you, sir," Lyndon replied more formally. He came to a stop at the foot of the stairs and snapped off a precise salute, then stood still with his hands clasped behind his back.

"At ease," the man added, and Lyndon nodded his thanks and shifted position slightly, moving his hands to clasp them in front instead. "This is Connor Connelly—" he paused "—as if you didn't know." He chuckled and the other man in the raised area joined in briefly.

"Yes sir." Lyndon allowed himself a small smile of acknowledgment and at last turned his eyes and full attention to the tall, lean man whose presence had dominated the room since the moment the young officer had entered it. "How do you do, sir?"

Connor Connelly stood and stepped lightly down the set of stairs until he was level with Lyndon. The man could have been in his forties, but Lyndon knew he was closer to seventy. His close-cropped curls were just as authentic-looking as if they were his natural head of hair.

The dusting of white strands here and there, more prominent at the temples, was a deliberate affectation. No one expected even moderately wealthy older people to let their hair turn gray. It was the same with the few lines that creased the sides of his mouth and corners of his eyes and lined his forehead. Someone of his stature and unimaginable wealth could have it all wiped away if he didn't want it there.

And indeed, the caramel-colored skin of his face, smooth and unmarred, had been very well tended. So yes, the signs of age he kept were of his own choosing.

"Lyndon, very nice to meet you," he said in a rich, mellifluous voice that was as instantly recognizable as his face. Although his eyes contained a haunted, pained expression, he managed to sound pleasant and professional. "Commander Stoughton tells me you're the best of the best."

"Thank you, sir, I'm glad the Commander thinks so," Lyndon said, flicking his eyes to Stoughton with a nod. He'd graduated top of his class and received praise from Stoughton at the time, but he didn't think someone as high up as him had been paying any attention to him as he worked his way through his probationary term of service.

Stoughton came down the steps and joined them. "He is," he replied to Connelly. "He's just starting out, but he's incredibly adaptable. We've been moving him around to different assignments and he's excelled at all of them. You're in narcotics now, aren't you, Bates?"

"Yes sir," Lyndon said, trying not to look startled that he knew.

"Bates also scored unusually high in traditional detective techniques at the academy," Stoughton told Connelly. "This case requires someone who can be effective without the aid of technology or weapons, and that's exceedingly rare these days." Lyndon's curiosity grew as he listened.

"And he's at the height of physical fitness," Stoughton continued. "He'll have no problem landing on his feet after selfing."

Lyndon couldn't keep surprise from showing on his face at that. He didn't comment but his mind was racing. Selfing? No one had told him. Why?

Stoughton saw the look on his face and smiled. "That's right; you up for a little adventure?"

It wasn't really a question, but Lyndon responded, "Yes, Commander." His voice was calm but he felt a growing excitement and trepidation as the reality hit him.

Stoughton's demeanor now turned grave and sympathetic. "Of course you know why you're here, even if you didn't know exactly what you'd be tasked with doing. This thing with Ms. Connelly—" He shifted his eyes to the older man. "Well, Connor, I don't have the words for how badly I feel—everyone on Earth feels about what happened to your daughter. But we're going to do everything we can to bring her killer to justice."

Connelly nodded, his calm voice belied by the pain in his eyes. "I appreciate it, and I trust your choice for the assignment." He looked at Lyndon. "You'll get this done, right, kid?"

"Yes sir," Lyndon said promptly. Although his mind was still buzzing with unanswered questions, he added, "I won't rest until I find who did this."

Connelly smiled. "You sound just like a movie character," he said in a gently kidding voice. "Let me get a look at you." He circled Lyndon, who stood perfectly still in his at-ease pose. "You're a good-looking guy, too. Very tasty, actually. You could have a future in acting—or even get your own show!"

Lyndon thought that sounded preposterous, but then again, Connor Connelly had a way of turning unlikely concepts into monster hits. From the show that was entirely about his daughter's privileged adventures and antics, to another that had as its main subject the eccentric, flamboyant ruler of the planet Mars, his current chart-toppers tended to be reality shows about one strong, love-or-hate personality—although he'd produced shows of all kinds in his long career.

Despite his obvious sorrow, Connelly was having fun expanding on his impulsive comment. "We could call it 'Lyndon's Law.' No wait—what's your last name? Bates? 'Unabated'!"

Lyndon felt the man's eyes travel up and down him and tried not to shift self-consciously. Connelly's prolific dating of both young women and men was as much a part of his public persona as his massive wealth and Midas touch at creating popular programs. At awards shows and society events, he generally traveled with an entourage of beautiful creatures jockeying to drape themselves on him, and his mansion was notorious for its hedonistic parties and constant supply of ready and willing playmates for him and his guests.

Stoughton chuckled, sounding relieved that he didn't have to maintain the somber tone he'd adopted but clearly impatient to move onto business. "Well, stardom will have to wait until Lyndon's back from Halcyon," he said.

"Let's give him a quick run-down of the case, and then he can get more background during the selfing process." He added, to Lyndon, "I don't know how much you know about it, but it takes a couple hours. Good news is you stay awake during it these days, so I can get you up to speed on the case file while you wait."

Lyndon nodded, relieved that Connelly's assessing gaze had been broken. He was used to getting admiring looks, but not from one of the richest and most powerful men in the galaxy, and he hadn't expected to encounter that kind of attention while being assigned to the most high-profile murder case in recent memory.

Stoughton continued. "As you know, Ms. Connelly was—the incident happened on Halcyon. Not at the resort, but on convent grounds. Now, no one but the nuns themselves are allowed to set foot in there. Everything is taken care of by them: gardening, food preparation, maintenance, construction, medical care, even law enforcement." Lyndon nodded. The convent's secrecy was well-known because of its contrast to the galaxy-renowned spa that coexisted on the planet.

"Ordinarily, they wouldn't allow outsiders from another planet in," Stoughton went on. "But the president was able to get a special dispensation from the Mother Superior. Owing to Crenshaw and Connor's stature" — he nodded deferentially to Connelly, who took it in stride — "as well as the severity of the crime, she realizes she needs to cooperate to avoid a diplomatic disaster."

Lyndon nodded, raptly attentive.

"But there was one thing she insisted on: Absolutely no man was going to set foot inside those walls. Well, we'd already identified you as our best prospect. Connor had heard all about you, and he didn't want anyone else. Plus, it doesn't hurt that you don't have any family or partner to think of, since we don't know how long you'll be away."

Lyndon winced inwardly but kept his face stoic. He had never managed to keep a steady relationship with any woman going for very long. His longest one, a two-year stint of dating that never progressed to living together—nor even in spending the night together most of the time—had ended a couple of months ago, in a heated argument over the amount of time and passion he put into his burgeoning career at the expense of everything else. The words "emotional void" may have been used by his ex.

Since then he'd put dating out of his mind and flung himself into making the best possible impression during his trial service in the National Police.

Stoughton continued, mercifully interrupting that chain of thought. "And thanks to Connor's selfer, we don't need to find a plan B." He paused and voiced what Lyndon had by now pieced together. "So you'll be going to Halcyon, but not as yourself."

Lyndon opened his mouth to speak, but couldn't think of what he was trying to say. Finally he nodded. "Yes sir," he said. "When do we get started?"

"The equipment is right in this building, so we'll begin immediately, unless you have any business to tend to or loose ends to tie up before you go."

"No sir," Lyndon said, without hesitation this time.

CHAPTER FOUR

Lyndon was swept back down in the elevator several floors to where Connelly kept his selfer. He'd seen the devices in photos and videos but never in real life. Only a few immensely wealthy people were able to afford their own selfer. They were seen as extravagant toys, strange new technology that had yet to be adopted by law enforcement.

Stoughton left him in the hands of a young man in an immaculate white uniform with a promise to come back once the process was under way. "Any questions before we start?" the attendant asked.

Lyndon had many questions, but most of them would best be answered by going through with it, he thought. "Will it be painful?" he asked.

"No," the attendant said. "Once you're in your new self, you may experience temporary disorientation, limb weakness, a loss of balance, but no one has ever complained about pain."

"Can I see my new body before I'm in it?"

The attendant shook his head. "I'm afraid that's strictly against protocol. We used to give people that option, but many found it extremely disturbing, and either couldn't go through with the process or struggled to adapt once the process was complete. The self is a fully laboratory-grown human body, but it doesn't have its own brain or personality, so until it's in use, it—you know the uncanny valley concept, right?"

Lyndon nodded impatiently. The human revulsion to too-realistic imitations of humans was common knowledge—it was why there were hardly any androids being made anymore. As they'd gotten more and more lifelike, the backlash had grown, and now they were deeply unpopular, even feared.

The young man continued. "I know you're probably of stronger stock than most, but I wouldn't want to jeopardize your assignment in any way." Lyndon didn't object, though he was now even more wildly curious to see the humanoid shell he was about to take over.

The attendant handed him a small folded piece of cloth, gestured to a door, and instructed him to remove all his clothes and put it on. In the small closet-like changing room, he removed and carefully straightened each piece of his uniform, tucking his briefs underneath the trousers, out of sight, and rolling his socks into small balls which he stuffed into each shoe. He wondered when he'd next put them back on, and where they'd stay.

When he shook out the provided garment, he saw that it was like a loose art smock, but made of a material he'd never encountered. It felt light and flimsy but stiff at the same time, and seemed slightly translucent. He pulled it over his head and used velcro strips to fasten the sides. The hem ended mid-thigh. His body couldn't be seen in detail through the material, but it was more revealing than he expected.

When he returned to the main area, the attendant instructed him to step into the selfer. He stood on two discs and fitted his arms and legs into indentations, then leaned his head back into the space reserved for it. The attendant tapped a nearby screen and the white plastic device adjusted itself until every part fit perfectly around him. Then the machine lifted him off the floor and reclined back at about a forty-five-degree angle.

Lyndon instinctively tried raising his head but realized it was gently restrained by the plastic now molded to him. He forced himself to relax, trying not to give in to the trapped feeling that suddenly flooded his body and made him want to struggle to free himself.

"Now I'm going to hook you up to monitors, feeding tubes, and a catheter," the attendant explained. "You'll be unconscious once you're fully selfed, or rather your consciousness will be elsewhere. You'll be breathing independently, but we'll have oxygen on standby just in case, and you'll be monitored around the clock."

He finished inserting the needles and tubes and taping everything down. "Comfortable?" he asked. Lyndon nodded. "Good. Now you'll be awake for the next couple hours; we map everything else to your self first. Your consciousness is the last to go, and it'll be like flipping a switch."

He tapped his fingers on a small touch screen on the side of the machine, and a trilling sound apparently signaled the beginning of the process. Lyndon didn't feel any different, though he was hyperfocused on trying to detect what was happening.

"I'll be monitoring the progress from the next room, but unless I need to adjust anything, you won't see me until you're in your new self!" The young man smiled and Lyndon tried to return it, mostly successfully.

The attendant left the room and Lyndon stared at the smooth white ceiling, feeling nothing except the claustrophobia of being trapped in the comfortable clutches of the machine. He puzzled over the scant information he'd been given until Stoughton entered a few minutes later.

In the presence of the National Police Commander, Lyndon noticed the strangeness of his situation—feeling exposed and helpless—even more acutely. If Stoughton felt out of his element, he didn't show it. He nodded a greeting as he approached Lyndon imprisoned in the selfer, as if it were entirely normal. "Still feeling all right about this assignment, officer?"

"Yes sir, absolutely. Only …"

"What is it, son?" Stoughton asked impatiently.

"Well, I was thinking … why is the selfer necessary? Not that I mind, but … wouldn't it be simpler just to say I was a woman? You know, trans?"

Stoughton nodded his understanding. "You'd think, but no. You'll find out, I think, that Halcyon is a very different world from ours, backward in some ways. Their view of sex—at least in terms of who they let into the convent—is rigid and biologically based. And you wouldn't make a convincing cisgender female in your own body."

Lyndon considered that with wonder and disgust. It was hard to imagine such a misguided mindset in present day.

"Anyway," Stoughton said in a businesslike tone. "Let's get you as ready as we can for this assignment." He pulled out a small mobile device and with a few taps, a holoscreen appeared in Lyndon's line of vision.

"Now, this victim isn't your usual case; you probably already know more about her than you ever wanted to know. But we're gonna go through normal protocol and start this case off on the right foot, because we can't have any screw-ups. Got it?"

"Yes sir," Lyndon said, sliding his eyes over to Stoughton since his head couldn't move.

Stoughton gestured at the screen and Lyndon turned his attention back to it. A still image of arguably the best-known face in the galaxy appeared.

"Our victim, Crenshaw Connelly. Twenty-four years old. Profession: star of the reality show 'Living la Vida Crenshaw.' Five-five, one hundred twenty pounds, of Caucasian and African American descent. Black hair, hazel eyes. Criminal record: two convictions for reckless driving, one for assault."

Stoughton chuckled. "Had a spat with another reality star when she was eighteen. Possibly cooked up for the show." He clicked to an image of Connor Connelly. "Family: father and mother, long divorced. Connor won the custody battle and Crenshaw hasn't been close with her mother since. No siblings, no spouses, no children."

He clicked through a series of photos of young men. "Significant others: none, though she leaves a trail of brokenhearted men wherever she goes. No special animosity from any past lovers that we've turned up, and as you know, she spends a lot of her life being videoed, so we'd know if any of them was harassing her."

The screen switched to a video that panned through cavernous buildings with steam rooms and saunas; past outdoor pools with crystal clear water tumbling down rocks; into leafy groves with seating seemingly coaxed out of the earth, rocks, and trees. Beautiful people strolled, relaxed, and frolicked.

"Halcyon Resort. Named after the planet it's on, which is named after the convent that's also there. The Sisters of Halcyon, originally hailing from Earth, bought this entire planet over a century ago, thanks to a wealthy believer who left her entire estate to the nuns, and named it after their existing religious order.

"Of course it was hard to find ways to make money for necessities they couldn't get on the planet itself, so they opened the spa. The Halcyon nuns are known to live extremely long, healthy lives and barely age visibly, so it's become one of the most expensive, exclusive resorts in the galaxy."

He flipped to two photos that could have been of the same dark-haired woman, though it was impossible to tell for sure; the first was out of focus, and in the second, the woman was turned away so only part of her profile was visible.

"This is the original and current Mother Superior. The one on the left is the one that negotiated the purchase of the planet and led her order there. On the right, the woman who runs it today. Rumors are it's the same person. I can't say for sure because there aren't any clear photographs, nor any fingerprints or DNA on file for either. Analysis of what we do have suggests a similar facial structure, but it's hard to believe—it'd make her at least a hundred fifty years old, maybe more. But some of the most loyal resort patrons believe it— want to, anyway."

Next appeared a still shot of a stone wall, blank white except for light swirls of green and blue, photographed at a distance across a grassy meadow.

"Halcyon the convent. When the religious order was based on Earth it was a fairly conventional religion, kind of an amalgamation of a few you've heard of—bit of Catholicism, neo-Paganism, Naturology—and they were open about their practices. But as soon as they moved operations to the planet Halcyon, they cut off all access to their inner workings. This is the only available view of the convent—the outer wall.

"Curious tourists drive up from the resort from time to time. If they get any farther than where this photo was shot from, they get detained, devices confiscated and photos deleted, and they get a nice friendly escort back to the resort proper. We've looked everywhere—there are no photos or videos of anything inside these walls. Well, until now, but I'll get to that in a second."

The screen changed from the shot of the convent outer wall to a video of Crenshaw talking excitedly into a camera, though it was on silent so Lyndon couldn't hear what she was saying. Stoughton continued. "The sisters never let people film on their planet, so it was a big deal when Crenshaw got them to allow her to bring 'La Vida' to the spa. According to Connor, his company paid an exorbitant fee for the privilege."

What followed was a series of clips from the show. Lyndon recognized many of them. You didn't have to try and watch Crenshaw's show; you could even try to avoid it, but it permeated every part of media and you ended up seeing at least the most talked-about segments. People's views of her ranged from adoration to disgust, and everything in between, but everyone knew who she was.

Lyndon himself was somewhere in the middle, right around mild annoyance. She was drop-dead gorgeous, and he sometimes couldn't resist watching just to see her don a barely-there bikini—as she had in several scenes at the resort—or tuning in to her more provocative stunts, like when she'd worked with a zero-gravity stripper to learn her craft.

But even a stunner like Crenshaw got old when it seemed like there was no choice but to see her everywhere.

That wouldn't be an issue anymore, at least not once the media circus settled down. He was surprised at the pang of sadness he felt to think she was gone now. Maybe it was just because nobody that young deserved to die. Or maybe familiarity had bred a certain amount of affection after all.

Stoughton continued, interrupting Lyndon's train of thought. "She filmed there for three days. Her only crew was this man." The screen switched to a view of a scruffy, skinny guy who could have been a teenager or in his forties, with rumpled brown hair and a goatee.

"Jinx Logan, her cameraman for the past five years. Whenever she went somewhere with only a skeleton crew, he was her guy. They both had those camera implants, so they didn't have to carry any equipment around. They control the camera with their eyes, and touching their heads—I don't know too much about the technical details." Lyndon tried not to let his impatience show. Stoughton acted like the technology was brand new, but camera implants had been in wide use for years.

"Anyway, everything's going along fine at first, and they're streaming footage to their studio to be edited overnight and broadcast the following day. The night of the third day, though—that was two days ago—" He fell silent and flipped to a different shot, what seemed like a still close-up photograph of a grassy field, so close you could see the individual blades. The two men stared at the screen, not speaking.

Suddenly the picture started moving, and Lyndon realized it was a video, not a still photograph. Stoughton turned on the sound with a slight movement of his finger. The blades of grass rustled as they moved and receded a few inches, then the camera panned jerkily to the left.

There was a blurred second where Lyndon couldn't make out anything, and then a young woman's face came into view. Her expression changed from horror to surprise, and she looked up, her chin becoming the dominant feature visible on the screen. Stoughton turned up the volume just in time for Lyndon to hear her shouts, echoing through the selfing chamber: "It's Crenshaw Connelly! I think she's dead!"

Stoughton paused the video and it froze on the strange angle of the woman's face. "And there you have it," he said with a heavy sigh. "The only known video ever taken inside the walls of Halcyon.

"If Crenshaw took any video while she was alive that night, she wasn't streaming it back to Earth. We haven't had a chance to see her body; the Mother Superior says she's got it in cold storage where it hopefully won't decompose, but we don't know the condition of the camera.

"At some point it kicked back into auto-transmitting mode; we think maybe when some trauma to the body jostled the machinery, or maybe there's a sort of black box emergency setting; we're contacting the manufacturer to find out, but it doesn't really matter how it happened. These few minutes of footage were sent to Earth. It recorded for about five minutes after she died, we think, but it's powered by the body, so once hers shut down completely, so did the camera."

He flipped back to the picture of Jinx. "Logan was captured outside the grounds of the convent. He's being held at the resort. We've questioned him remotely, and he was able to tell us how she snuck in, but nothing of value as to who killed her and why. Still, you'll get a chance to talk to him in person once you get there. Maybe a couple days in lockup will give him time to think of something he left out."

The screen disappeared and Lyndon turned his eyes to Stoughton, who shrugged. "This is where I'd show you photos of the crime scene, but that bit of footage is all we have right now. The convent police haven't been very communicative if they've gathered any evidence, and of course we don't even have any regular pics or video inside the convent.

Damn place is the best kept secret in the known galaxy. It's a miracle, frankly, that they're letting us in there voluntarily.

"But they've never had an incident on this level on their planet before. How could there have been? There's no one more famous than Crenshaw Connelly, and no private citizen more powerful than Connor. They're scared Earth will force our way in if they don't let us, that's what I think." He pocketed his mobile device.

"So my point is, you've got to tread very lightly. Whatever weird rules or laws they may have, you do whatever you can to not violate them. This is a very delicate situation that could easily get out of hand. And whatever you do, don't let them know you're really male." He stared intently at Lyndon. "I'm not exaggerating. The peace between our planets is depending on you."

"Yes sir," Lyndon said, with as much confidence as he could muster. "I understand."

Stoughton checked the screen on the side of the selfer. "This part is almost over, looks like," he said. "Once you get into that new body, Connor's man will explain how everything works." He smiled despite himself. "I couldn't tell you; I've never seen one of these things up close. This is pretty cool, actually." Lyndon tried to smile back.

Just then a beeping sound started emanating from the machine. "Good luck, Bates," Stoughton said. "I'll come see you when you wake up."

Lyndon began to feel a rising panic, but he forced it back with all the strength of his will. "Thank you, sir," he said. The beeping became more frequent, then a steady keening sound. Lyndon instinctively strained to look around, but could only lie still. When he blacked out, it was instantaneous.

* * *

Lyndon awoke, forcing his reluctant eyes open. He was no longer in the selfer; he was lying prone on an impossibly soft surface that cradled his body. He stirred and realized he was still restrained, this time by wide soft plastic cuffs on his wrists and ankles and bands around his forehead and waist. His heart hammered with a fight-or-flight urgency, but he forced himself to stop struggling against the restraints.

The light was dimmer than it had been. He flicked his eyes from side to side and realized he was in a different room. He was still clothed in the odd material; he could tell by how it felt on his skin. Just then, at the edge of his peripheral vision, the attendant approached.

The man's gaze seemed different somehow, but his tone remained the same, impersonal and calm. "How are you feeling, Lyndon?"

Lyndon searched for words. The act of speaking was suddenly difficult. Finally he managed. "A little weird." He gasped in shock at the sound of his voice.

Her voice.

CHAPTER FIVE

The attendant seemed unfazed by the new voice. "Well, your vitals look great." He felt Lyndon's pulse. "Elevated heartbeat, but not like you're being rejected by the body, or having a panic attack. Are you feeling calm enough for me to take these restraints off?"

Lyndon nodded, not ready to hear herself speak again just yet. The attendant searched her face, assessing. One motion out of Lyndon's view, and all of the plastic bands parted at once. Lyndon sat up, swinging her legs around so they dangled from the side of whatever it was she was on—a larger version of a doctor's examining table, with more cushioning.

But Lyndon wasn't interested in the bed; she was interested in her legs, still muscled but differently shaped, feet and toes smaller and more slender. She put her hands on her face, running her fingertips over her skin and marveling at the smoothness; even with laser-shaving every morning there had always been a hint of roughness on the jaw, but not anymore.

She drew her hands down and looked at them, turning them back and forth. Then she became aware of the attendant standing watching her, and forced her attention back to him.

"Sorry," she said.

He smiled and shook his head. "Not at all. It's always a bit of an adjustment to enter a new body, and this is the most drastic transformation I've ever taken part in." He checked an invisible screen next to him. "We've kept you nearly the same height, five-eight, so you'll be tall for a woman but not so much that you'll draw undue attention. You're thirty pounds lighter, so that's going to feel strange as you walk around. Your muscles are smaller but substantial; this body's in fighting form." His smile widened. Lyndon instinctively tightened various muscles and felt their strength. "Are you ready to see your boss now?"

"Yeah, I guess so," Lyndon said. The attendant went to the door and stepped outside, letting in Commander Stoughton.

"Well, I'll be damned," the Commander said when he saw Lyndon. "Is that really you, Officer Bates?"

"Yes sir, it's me," she said, as much in awe of her transformation as Stoughton seemed to be. Oddly she felt less exposed; her body felt so alien to her that she felt removed from the fact of the faintly translucent mesh gown that barely reached mid-thigh.

Stoughton looked her up and down, shaking his head admiringly. "I had my doubts this would really work, even though Connor assured me it would. But I would never think

you weren't a woman if I didn't know better."
He looked in Lyndon's eyes. "You feel all
right?"

"Yeah—yes sir. A little dazed, but I'm
getting better."

"Good, good," Stoughton said. He couldn't
seem to tear his eyes away from Lyndon, but
reluctantly he said, "Well, I'd better leave you
alone so you can get acclimated and get ready
for your transportation to Halcyon." He held
out his hand. Lyndon shook it, then snapped as
smart a salute as she could manage in her off-
kilter state.

Stoughton left and the attendant came back
in. "We've got a range of clothing for you to
choose from and a private apartment for you to
change in. You'll have a few hours to get
acclimated to your body so you aren't
stumbling around like a baby deer." He
laughed, and Lyndon did a little too, still
surprised at the sound of her own voice.

"You've accepted the body amazingly well,
so it shouldn't take long before it feels almost
normal to move around in. Really there's

nothing more to know; it operates like a regular human body. Of course there are some—fundamental differences from your real body, but you'll adjust to those quickly enough." He looked slightly embarrassed but moved on quickly. "Any questions?"

Lyndon shook her head, unable to turn any of the bewilderment in her mind into articulate questions. The attendant handed her a bathrobe. "Well, then, I'll show you where you'll be staying until you're ready to be transported to Halcyon."

* * *

In the living room of the luxurious apartment, a few floors up from the selfing rooms, Lyndon was left alone. She stood still, shell-shocked by everything that had happened. She couldn't describe even to herself how she felt. Like she was still Lyndon but someone completely different at the same time.

As soon as the attendant had closed the door, she'd done what she'd been thinking about almost since she woke up—put her hand to her crotch. Feeling the small mound there instead of the male genitalia she'd had all her life was profoundly unsettling and she'd pulled her hand away almost immediately.

Finally she roused herself from her stupor and found the bedroom of the apartment. Looking through the full closet, she chose a pair of slacks and a long-sleeve top and threw them on the bed. The dresser next to it contained undergarments and socks. She held up a bra as if she'd never seen one before. She'd taken them off girls many times, never put one on herself.

Shrugging off her bathrobe, she unfastened the sides of the odd smock-like garment and lifted it over her head. Just then she caught a glimpse of herself in a full-length mirror and gasped. The smock fell forgotten to the floor.

Lyndon moved closer to the mirror, hardly believing her own appearance. She put her hand to the side of her face as if to make sure the reflection wasn't a trick. She had short dark blond hair still, though a couple inches longer than how she kept it on her real body. Her eyes still looked blue, but the shape was entirely different. That was where the resemblance ended. A stranger looked back at her from the mirror.

Her hand moved down the side of her face and neck and onto her chest. She watched herself in disbelief as her hands slid up to cup her new breasts, on the small side but perfectly formed. She was unprepared for the strength of sensation as she brushed her nipples. The lightest movement on them sent shivery waves of arousal coursing through her entire body.

Her breathing quickened and her vision blurred. One hand moved down to the small patch of hair between her legs and this time she didn't shy away, but found the spot that was aching to be touched.

She slipped her fingers lower and felt a gathering moisture there. Bathing her fingertips in it she returned to the clitoris. Watching herself in the mirror was disorienting, yet she couldn't look away or help but become even more aroused at the strange sight.

In no time at all she felt something building, similar to what she'd experienced in the past yet completely alien, until she felt as if she burst open. With a ragged sigh, she fell back onto the bed, eyes closed, marveling at the aftershock that ebbed through her in gradually receding, throbbing waves.

CHAPTER SIX

The trip had taken minutes once Lyndon had dressed, packed, and entered the transporter in Connelly's building. After a few seconds of nothingness she emerged in a similar device in a plain-looking room.

A male attendant stood at the ready. As soon as she appeared, he smiled and reached out to help her down, his hand and expression gentle and attentive in a way that Lyndon hadn't experienced before.

"Officer Bates," he said, looking at an invisible screen to the side of the transport platform. "You're right on time, and your escort will be here shortly." He took her by the elbow and guided her into another room. Lyndon couldn't help but notice the starkly different way she was being treated, the cavalier way she was touched and led places as if she were incapable of walking in a straight line by herself.

She was led into a lobby where a few other people waited, seemingly for their turn to transport back to Earth, because a name was called and a man got up to follow the same attendant. She noticed he merely nodded and gestured in the direction of the transport platforms, rather than taking the passenger by the arm.

"Just arrived?" a voice close to her asked. She smelled the liquor on the man's breath almost as soon as he spoke.

"That's right," Lyndon said neutrally.

"Beautiful place," the man slurred rapturously. "My first time, but I know I'm gonna be back." He looked pointedly down the v-neck of Lyndon's shirt, then up at her face. "Acshally, maybe I should extend my stay now instead." He leaned even closer. "I can show you the wonders of the resort. Healing baths for two, private rest'rant booths 'n' everything."

Lyndon was too bemused to know how to react. "Uh, I uh, appreciate the offer, but—"

"Come on, sweetie," the man said confidingly. "I'll pay for everything." He put a hand on Lyndon's knee. "We'll get to know each other real well."

Lyndon resisted the urge to punch the stranger. "I'm gonna need you to take your hand off me, sir," she said briskly.

The man's ingratiating expression disappeared, replaced by an ugly scowl. "Uptight bitch," he said. "What's your problem anyway? You should be grateful anyone finds your skinny ass attractive."

Lyndon had been given strict orders not to reveal herself as an Earth police officer outside the convent itself, so as not to bring any more attention to the case than was necessary. She moved the man's hand from her knee with a firm gesture, and stood up to wait elsewhere in the lobby. She felt a sharp blow on her rear and spun around, anger flaring up as the drunk man leered at her, looking pleased with himself.

She was on the verge of hauling the man up by his shirt collar and charging him with assaulting an officer, orders be damned, when another name was called and the man stumbled off in the direction of the transport room, looking back at her to mouth "bitch" one more time.

"Officer Bates?" She turned to see a breathtakingly pretty woman in a flowing velvety ankle-length garment.

"Yes, that's me," Lyndon replied.

"I'll take you to meet the Mother Superior," the woman said. Her tone was businesslike and didn't invite conversation, so Lyndon followed her silently outside and into a driverless car. After several minutes the car stopped at a small sheltered station with the convent in view, and they walked the rest of the way, a few hundred yards across open grass.

The green- and blue-tinged white marbled walls seemed unbroken until the nun touched a spot that looked like everywhere else, and a door slid silently open. Lyndon followed her silent companion across another expanse of green lawn and along an enclosed walkway. She was deposited in a large office, where a woman in similar but more intricately decorated robes stood up from a large chair and came around from behind her desk.

"Thank you for coming," the woman said. "I am the Mother Superior of Halcyon." She spoke politely, though there was an undercurrent of tension in her tone, and held out her hand to shake Lyndon's. "I'm aware of how vital it is for Earth to find a satisfactory resolution to this unfortunate incident," she continued, "so I'm very glad you're here."

She was a stunning but intimidating woman of indeterminate age and race, with smooth olive skin and straight, glossy black hair pulled back in a tight bun. "I'll introduce you to your servant and show you around a little. Then she can take you to your room to get settled before starting your investigation."

Servant? Lyndon wondered. But before she could say anything, the nun pulled a long rope made of soft green material suspended from the ceiling, and a bell chimed somewhere.

Almost immediately another woman, perhaps in her early twenties, entered the room. Lyndon couldn't help noticing the ripe curves of her body, evident even under the coarse-looking fabric of her loose beige knee-length dress—a sharp contrast to the soft ankle-length garment worn by the Mother Superior. Her long wavy hair was gathered in a loose ponytail at the nape of her neck.

Except for a quick glance at Lyndon, her eyes remained downcast, her hands folded in front of her. She approached the two women and knelt down on the floor in front of them, her head bent.

Barely glancing at her, the Mother Superior addressed Lyndon. "Pella will be yours for the duration of your stay. She's a postulant, so someday, hopefully"—her tone took on a mild severity—"she'll become a nun herself." She raised her eyebrows. "How much were you taught about our order before you came?"

"Not much, ma'am," Lyndon said truthfully, still marveling at her new voice. "There isn't much information available about you."

The Mother Superior nodded approvingly. "We prefer it that way, but you'll need some information to be able to navigate your stay here. When a young woman wants to join our order, she must first be a postulant for at least ten years. Postulants learn humility and self-control—and demonstrate their dedication to our order—through absolute obedience during this period.

"It is an important part of her religious growth, so please be firm with her, and with every postulant you encounter. They exist only to serve and strive to have no will of their own, so you must tell them when to speak and what you want them to do."

She raised a hand and extended her index finger upward. "A few absolute laws I must tell you about, since you're a newcomer: There must be no physical or verbal abuse of our postulants, ever. If they disobey, which is extremely rare, their punishment is automatically administered, and either we'll make sure they rectify the situation to your satisfaction or we'll replace them with someone more to your liking."

Lyndon broke in, shocked. "Of course not! I would never—"

The Mother Superior smiled and nodded but cut her short. "And our other absolute rule: Never initiate sexual relations with them, please." She saw Lyndon's aghast face and shrugged. "We don't require celibacy of our members, nor are we naive. But there can't be any such conduct between postulants and their superiors. Since they have no free will, there's no way for them to give consent."

Lyndon felt her face get hot. She looked down at Pella and was very glad the girl's head was bent so her face wasn't visible. "I promise you, I'm here in an official capacity, and I had no intention—"

The Mother Superior waved her objections away. "I believe you. I didn't think either issue was a concern, but not everyone has had a servant who is required to do everything they say, so I wanted to make sure you knew the parameters. Other than that, she's under your command." Finally she looked down at Pella. "Stand, girl."

Pella got to her feet, eyes still downcast. "Look at us, girl," the Mother Superior said. She raised her eyes and looked first at the nun and then at Lyndon. A cautious smile hovered on the young woman's lips. "You may speak."

"It's nice to meet you, Miss," she said, her voice pretty and friendly despite sounding a little rusty with disuse. Her words sounded as though she'd rehearsed them in her head. "Please let me make your stay here as comfortable as possible. Anything you need, just tell me." She fell silent again and dropped her eyes.

"All right," the Mother Superior said briskly. "Before we go, one other note." She gestured toward her desk and a computer screen appeared in the air. "Our order eschews technology for the most part, but for practicality's sake, I do use it to conduct some interplanetary business and monitor the resort. Normally this is the only room that has any technology, but I'm allowing an exception. We've added connectivity to the apartment where you'll be staying, so you'll be able to use yours only within those rooms. We only ask that you leave your devices in there and don't bring them onto the grounds."

Lyndon nodded reluctantly. "I understand, ma'am."

The Mother Superior reached out to Pella and lifted her chin. Around the girl's neck was a thin black band, a visual anomaly against her hand-crafted clothing and unadorned natural hair. "This is the only other technology we use," she said.

"In the early days of our order, ensuring our postulants' total adherence to their rules of conduct required constant vigilance by the nuns. Eventually we decided it would be infinitely easier on us, freeing up our time to go about our business, if we allowed this solution onto the grounds."

She pushed a button and a number 5 lit up on the collar-like device. "This tracker monitors everything including her speech, her actions, where she goes, and her bedtime, and alerts our governing body to any infractions. It also tracks how many years of servitude are left."

She took her hand away and Pella's head dropped again. "It puts the responsibility for their obedience entirely in their own hands, which saves time and energy. And nuns would occasionally feel conflicted about whether to report something that seemed unintentional or less serious. This takes that moral dilemma out of the picture."

The Mother Superior ordered Pella to take Lyndon's bags—Lyndon bit back the urge to object—and they left the chamber and stepped out onto the grounds.

CHAPTER SEVEN

The air had a freshness and quality of vitality that was almost indescribable compared with what Lyndon was used to on Earth. The sun-dappled grass rippled with a light breeze. Here and there nuns and postulants were gardening, cleaning, reading, or walking the grounds.

A few feet away, a circle of postulants sat on the grass, listening to a nun perched on a large mossy stone shaped almost like a chair. Lyndon couldn't hear what she was saying, but she was holding a thick, ancient book in her hand. Lyndon stared, fascinated by the artifact.

They approached a small pond with pristine-looking water, the pebbled bottom clearly visible. "It's beautiful here," Lyndon said.

The Mother Superior nodded with evident pride. "Generations of careful stewardship have helped us preserve the environment and even make improvements to our natural surroundings without disrupting the ecosystem." She didn't need to reference Earth for Lyndon to know she was comparing the two planets; for centuries, the home planet had faced nearly unceasing struggles to stave off climate catastrophe due to past mishandling.

A young woman in a rough postulant's dress approached the pond from the other side with a pitcher and dipped it in the crystal water to fill it. "Girl!" the Mother Superior called. The postulant looked up wide-eyed. "Get our guest a drink." The postulant bobbed her head, set the pitcher down, and ran off, reappearing less than a minute later with a glass.

She poured from the pitcher into the glass and handed it to Lyndon, curiosity blooming in her gaze. Lyndon thanked her and she backed away but, distracted, she tripped on a rock and nearly fell backward into the pond. "Oh no!" she blurted, but managed to catch herself and merely landed in a sitting position in the grass beside the water.

Instead of relief, the girl's face held a stricken expression. As she sat frozen, her collar gave out an insistent beep and lit up with the number 8, which flashed and changed to a 9. The girl's eyes filled with tears, but she stood up resolutely and went to retrieve her pitcher and take it wherever it was intended for.

"What just happened?" Lyndon asked, puzzled.

The Mother Superior sighed. "She spoke without being given permission to speak and therefore violated one of the rules of obedience. Any time there's an infringement, the tracker will add another year to their servitude. In this way, we make sure that cumulatively, there are at least ten complete years of perfect obedience, qualifying them to become a nun."

Lyndon tried to conceal her shock. A year's sentence for involuntarily crying out while tripping?

The Mother Superior looked more closely at Lyndon. "You seem uncomfortable, so I hope this will help put you at your ease. When I say our postulants have no free will, they do have control over one important thing: their ability to leave the order whenever they want, with absolutely no repercussions. If that girl feels that another year will be unbearable, she's free to leave immediately."

"Has anyone ever done that?" Lyndon asked.

"Oh yes," the Mother Superior replied. "Very seldom, but they have. We pay them fairly for however many years they've served, provide them transport to wherever it is they want to start over, and even put them in touch with resources to help retrain them for working in nonsecular life."

She seemed to have lost interest in giving a tour, or perhaps she'd remembered something she had to attend to. "I'll let you get to your quarters; Pella will show you where they are and help you settle in."

Lyndon shifted awkwardly. "It's really not necessary, you know; if you just direct me where to go I can take care of myself."

The Mother Superior frowned as if she weren't used to being contradicted. "You don't know your way around and you're likely unused to managing without technology. It'll save you much time and effort if you let me do this for you, so you can focus on the case and hopefully resolve it sooner."

Lyndon reluctantly relented. "I appreciate it, ma'am," she said somewhat unconvincingly.

But the Mother Superior wasn't finished. "And please, for Pella's sake, don't try and tempt or trick the poor girl into violations of her oath. As you've seen, there's no leniency in our system. And there's no limit to the number of years the tracker can add to her servitude. Help her stay on track to becoming the nun she wants to be." She looked at Pella severely. "Be careful, girl," she said. Pella nodded, looking suddenly nervous. "Go on, take Officer Bates to her quarters," the Mother Superior prompted, and she hurriedly picked up Lyndon's baggage and led the way down another walkway.

The building was on the other side of a large clearing from the one where the Mother Superior's office was located. Lyndon followed Pella under an arch, across a courtyard and to a door on the ground floor. She set the heavy bags down with a nearly imperceptible grunt and opened the door, stepping aside and looking expectantly at Lyndon, who walked past her into the room.

It was a small but cozy studio apartment, with a bed on one side of the room and a comfortable-looking armchair on the other, covered with a velvety fabric similar in appearance to the cloth of the nuns' garments. A bathroom and kitchen were visible through half-open doors.

Pella closed the door, then hauled the suitcases over to a closet. She knelt, opened them, and began putting clothes away.

Lyndon, embarrassed, followed her and tried to take over. "You don't have to do this. I'll take care of it, really."

Pella hesitated, then backed away on her knees. She sat with her head bent, silent, but it was evident from her breathing that she was crying.

Lyndon felt at a loss. "Pella, what's wrong?" she said. "Is everything okay?"

Pella looked up, her eyes welling with tears, wordless. Lyndon steeled herself. "You can speak," she said reluctantly. "Please be straight with me. What's wrong?"

Pella let out one muffled sob. "I want to do a good job for you, Miss," she managed, "but I'm not sure how to."

Lyndon wondered how she'd ever gotten in this situation. "I don't want to have a servant," she said uncomfortably. "I don't think it's right." Pella sat miserably, not saying anything.

Lyndon sighed. "Please speak," she said again. "How can I help you?"

Pella sniffled. "By letting me serve you, Miss," she said. "Otherwise I'm not doing what the Mother Superior told me to do, and not doing what I'm supposed to do."

Lyndon was at a loss. "I don't like doing this to you," she said starkly. When Pella didn't answer, she said again, "Speak."

Pella brought her breathing under control and seemed to carefully consider her words before she spoke. "Miss … if you let me do this, you'll help me get what I want. We're helping each other, okay?"

Lyndon thought about it. Finally she nodded. "Okay," she said. "Let's make a deal. I can handle everything else, but this not talking thing? It's fucked up. How about I make a blanket rule that you talk to me whenever you want to say anything? Other than that we can do this the way you want." She saw Pella's hand flutter to her throat. "That would be all right, right? Does that thing know if you talk to me that we've made a deal?"

Pella hesitated with her mouth slightly open. Finally she risked speaking. "I think so?" She and Lyndon both held their breath, but the collar didn't beep. After a few moments, they both smiled in relief.

Lyndon breathed a sigh. "Okay, so that's how it's gonna go," she said. "I'll try to be okay with all this special treatment you're giving me, and you promise to just talk to me."

Pella hesitated, then said in her rusty voice, "But maybe when others are around …?"

Lyndon caught her drift. "When we're around the nuns, we'll do it the other way. Okay?"

"Okay," Pella breathed. "Can I put your things away now, Miss?"

Lyndon smiled a little. "Yeah, okay," she said. "Thank you, Pella." She hesitated. "I don't suppose you'd be comfortable just calling me by my name?" She didn't want to explain that the "Miss" moniker was unnerving on several levels. And when she saw the look on Pella's face, she gave up. "Never mind. Forget I asked."

CHAPTER EIGHT

After Pella had finished putting everything away and Lyndon had checked in with headquarters, the two left the apartment. Lyndon had reluctantly placed her mobile in a drawer, marveling at how unmoored she felt without it.

Pella shut the door behind them and took an old-fashioned key from her pocket. She locked the door with it and handed it to Lyndon. Then her eyes widened and she reached back into her pocket, producing a small violet band that appeared to be of the same material as the black one around her neck.

She held it out wordlessly, then remembered she could speak unbidden. "I forgot to give you this, Miss," she said. "This connects to my tracker. It goes on your wrist and you can use it to summon me if you need me and I'm not around, like at night or if we get separated." She tapped it and showed Lyndon the few simple commands on it. "It'll tell me where you are so I can find you."

They can't have a regular electronic lock on the door, but they sure spare no technology to control their free labor, Lyndon thought dryly. She kept her observation to herself.

"Okay, thanks," she said simply, slipping the wristband over her left hand. It was so comfortable she almost immediately stopped noticing it was there. "Can you show me where Ms. Connelly's body was found? Is that on the way to where we're going?"

"Yes, Miss," Pella said. "It's not far from here." She brought Lyndon back past the small pond and the main buildings of the campus, and gestured at a patch of grass indistinguishable from the rest. Lyndon crouched and inspected the ground. It looked undisturbed.

She looked up at Pella. "Was the area cleaned after the body was moved?"

"I don't know for sure, Miss, but it has rained since that night."

Lyndon sighed and stood. There was nothing to be learned from this crime scene. "All right. Thanks, Pella. We can keep going."

Pella led the way through the grounds. She'd fallen back into her natural silence, so Lyndon prompted her with questions to get her talking. "What do you usually do around here, when you're not taking care of me?"

"I'm a domestic," Pella replied. "Housework, cleaning, serving food, stuff like that." She shrugged. "A lot of us do that, but some postulants get trained in a specific area, so they can take over certain roles when they become nuns. There are builders, farmers, nurses, security guards, chefs, all sorts of things. We don't bring in any outside help—"

she paused as she realized she was talking to an outsider—"I mean, except in special cases. So we have to have sisters trained in everything."

They walked past a nun and Pella clammed up, but once they were alone again she continued. "And then I spend time in religious education, of course, and our rites and services."

"What are those like?" Lyndon asked, mildly interested.

Pella hesitated. "We're forbidden to talk about our rites outside the convent, Miss. But in all things we honor and worship our goddess whom we call Gaeadana."

"Right," Lyndon said, searching her memory. "Mother Earth, sort of?"

"Yes," Pella said. "Our founder Callah became aware of the powerful sentient life force that sustains the universe, but she was nameless, beyond names in the way we think about them. So Callah combined two words for 'Mother Earth' from Greek and Celtic. We call our goddess Gaeadana because we needed a way to talk about her and focus our minds on her in worship."

"If she has no name, how do you know she's female?"

"Because she gave birth to and nurtures everything that is or ever will be," Pella said simply.

"Is that why only women are allowed in your order?"

She nodded. "We believe that only women can truly commune with Gaeadana, and the deepest connection isn't possible in the company of men."

Lyndon thought about asking if Pella felt that "deepest connection" at the moment but was afraid she wouldn't be able to contain her smirk, so she changed the subject.

"Were you one of the people who found the body?" Pella stiffened a little, then nodded again.

"It happened not far from my dorm. We heard these screams and came running out. I wasn't the one who actually found her though; that was Crystal." She shook her head sadly.

"She yelled without thinking and got another year."

Lyndon felt more indignation than Pella seemed to at the injustice. But thinking of the outburst she'd seen on the video prompted another question. "Crystal said 'It's Crenshaw Connelly.' If you don't have technology—much technology—in the convent, how did she recognize her?"

"Oh, everyone gets a little bit of television," Pella said matter-of-factly. "Sometimes we get taken out to the resort to help out the regular employees: fix things, clean rooms, that sort of thing. The other workers usually have shows on and we get to see them."

"So you're allowed off the grounds?"

"Yes, when it's necessary. We used to hardly ever go over there; the resort is staffed with outsiders, and there are men too, so, you know, it's discouraged to be around them." Lyndon felt a flash of guilt. "Especially postulants, you know, because of what the Mother Superior said, not being able to say yes or no, so we always have to have a nun watching us for our safety."

"You 'used to' go there less often?"

"Yeah, but I think they're short-staffed more often now, so our convent is taking on more of the work." She shrugged and smiled. "I like to go over there. It's basically the same stuff I do here but I get to watch TV sometimes while I work. And see other people. The guests are all so fancy, and some of the workers are really nice!"

Something in her voice made Lyndon look at her more closely, and she thought she saw a suppressed smile hovering on the postulant's lips.

"Anyone in particular?" Lyndon couldn't resist asking. The girl blushed and shrugged. "If you weren't a postulant—if you were already a nun—would you be allowed to date someone?"

"Not really," Pella said softly. "The nuns can—see people from time to time, outsiders or each other, but it can't turn into a relationship." She hesitated, then added, "We can be with each other, if that's what girls are into, because the only people we can give consent with are other postulants. As long as it doesn't get in the way of our duties or become a distraction." Lyndon was wildly curious, but Pella looked despondent and more than a little self-conscious, so she let it drop.

They'd walked quite a way during their talk and Lyndon hadn't been paying attention, so she felt completely lost as they approached a large bluish-white rock that jutted up from the ground about ten feet, and was perhaps twenty feet wide. Like all the organic elements she'd seen so far, it looked both natural and designed at the same time.

Pella pressed a hand to the rock and Lyndon suddenly noticed a seam running vertically along it. At the top, a horizontal line connected to it. Pella slipped a hand inside the seam and pulled, and a huge block of the stone swung forward, revealing a dark opening. Lyndon marveled at the smoothness of it, and how Pella was able to move it with seemingly little exertion.

"Another piece of technology, huh?" Lyndon asked cynically.

"No, it's not technology," Pella said without further elaboration, stepping inside and taking an old-fashioned lantern from a hook on the wall. She turned a knob on the side and a spark appeared, blossoming into a flame.

Lyndon stepped into the opening after her, still puzzling over the door as Pella swung it closed behind them.

The girl raised her lantern and led the way down a cool stone tunnel with rough-hewn walls and ceiling but a smooth floor. The dim light she was holding was more than adequate, magnified by the shimmering white rock around them.

The tunnel sloped down gradually, and the air cooled as they went lower. After a few minutes of walking, the hall led them into a chamber, lit by more lanterns hanging on the walls. There were shelves carved into the walls, cloth sacks bulging with unknown contents hanging from hooks, and wooden barrels and boxes stacked neatly along the sides.

But what drew Lyndon's attention was a stone slab near the middle of the space. It was covered by a clean, sturdy-looking cloth, draped over what was clearly a human body. Beyond it, the Mother Superior sat in a chair fashioned from the same wood as the crates in the room. She wore a serene and patient expression and stood unhurriedly as they approached.

"I trust you found your quarters satisfactory?" she asked Lyndon.

"Yes ma'am, thank you," Lyndon replied.

"And Pella? Is she making herself useful?"

"She's doing an outstanding job." Lyndon smiled at Pella, who beamed.

"I'm very pleased to hear it," the Mother Superior said briskly without a glance in the postulant's direction. She gestured around the chamber. "Please forgive these primitive surroundings. This is a cold-storage area for perishable foods. We don't have a morgue on our grounds, or even at the resort, so this was the best we could do. You must understand, death is rare on Halcyon, and a suspicious death even more so. We don't normally have a need to save a body for examination."

Lyndon nodded, frowning slightly as she took all that in. "I may have to ask for special dispensation to bring my mobile in here later and get a full body scan for our medical examiner back on Earth, but for now let's have a look at her and see what I can find out."

The Mother Superior also frowned, possibly at the prospect of more technology on the grounds. But she said nothing, merely pulled the cloth off the object it was shrouding.

CHAPTER NINE

Pella managed to keep her shocked reaction to a sharp intake of air, but turned away, hugging herself.

Lyndon, on the other hand, drew closer, staring down. She was surprised at the sorrow that arose in her. She'd participated in murder investigations during probationary service and usually had no trouble approaching bodies and crime scenes with detachment. She hadn't expected to feel sad to see a spoiled rich reality star's corpse.

But seeing the normally animated Crenshaw Connelly cold, lifeless, a grim grayish cast to her skin, was a shock. Her face still retained a certain beauty despite everything; her hair formed a soft cloud around her head, perfect except a few fragments of grass and leaves caught in the strands.

"I'll need to examine the wounds," Lyndon said, donning gloves. "Could you help me undress her, ma'am?" She pulled a second pair of gloves from her pocket and held them out to the Mother Superior.

The nun's face registered disgust for a moment before she rearranged her features to a more neutral expression. "Pella!" she said briskly. "Help undress the body."

Slowly and reluctantly, Pella approached. When Lyndon saw her face, she protested. "No, that's all right, Pella. I can handle it."

"Nonsense," the Mother Superior said sharply. "She'll help, or she'll do it herself."

Lyndon remembered what Stoughton had said about not challenging the cultural norms of the convent, and it was all that restrained her from arguing. Instead she tried to do as much as she could on her own, directing Pella to work on the shoes and socks while she worked off the hoodie, ripped in several places and stiff with dried blood. The catsuit looked impossible, so she asked for a knife, which Pella retrieved, and cut away the one-piece garment. A bra and underwear and socks still remained on the cadaver.

Large sections of the catsuit that Lyndon lifted away from her body were utterly rigid with copious amounts of blood. Underneath it, Crenshaw's skin was mottled and bruised-looking. There was one wound on her side; the scorched edges visible under the crusted blood indicated she'd been stabbed by a laser-blade.

But the video suggested she'd died face-down. Lyndon glanced at Pella's ashen face and began to lift the body herself. It was difficult with the rigor mortis that had set in. Her heart sank when she heard the Mother Superior's voice: "Pella! Help Officer Bates turn the body over."

The girl's trembling hands touched Crenshaw's leg gingerly while Lyndon lifted the body by the arm and waist. As Pella steeled herself and put her strength into it, they managed to turn the cold cadaver over. It settled heavily onto the slab, and the postulant skittered back with a barely suppressed scream. Lyndon sent her a pitying glance, but then her eyes were drawn to the body.

Here was where the majority of the damage had been done. Four more scorched stab wounds and more blood, though not as much as had soaked into the clothing, marred Crenshaw's smooth, slender back. Several more bruises showed signs of a struggle.

Lyndon reached for Crenshaw's hair close to her temple and parted it to her scalp, then in another place and another. Her fingers gently probed the dead girl's scalp until she found something. A tiny button under the skin. She pressed it and a small portion of scalp and skull clicked open. The Mother Superior and even Pella crowded in curiously to see it.

Lyndon peered closer, reaching in to retrieve something, but moved back. "It's not there," she said.

"What isn't?" the Mother Superior asked sharply.

"There's a backup drive installed in every internal camera. If Ms. Connelly was filming when she was attacked, it'd have that information stored, and our tech team could eventually retrieve it." She shook her head. "Maybe the killer got it. I can't imagine she'd be going around without that in there. Although I don't know very much about the technology, so I suppose it's a possibility." Lyndon sighed and closed the skull back up. "That could've been our best piece of evidence."

She looked up. "Since we don't have the backup drive, I'm going to need to do a full forensic scan. Mother Superior, may I have permission to bring my mobile here?"

The nun sighed. "I suppose so, if you must," she said. "You'll take it straight back to your room and leave it there when you're finished, of course."

"Thank you, ma'am," Lyndon said. "I'll do that later. First I want to question everyone who was there when the body was discovered. And then I'll need to speak with Ms. Connelly's cameraman, Jinx Logan."

"Of course," the Mother Superior said.

Lyndon gathered Crenshaw's clothing into a cloth bag that Pella retrieved and held open for her. The postulant drew it closed and held it firmly, so Lyndon didn't try to take it from her. Pella was instructed when and where to bring Lyndon to question the witnesses, and they left the Mother Superior as she covered the body with the cloth again.

Back at Lyndon's quarters, Pella fixed her a cup of fragrant herbal tea while the officer spread out the clothing on the floor of the studio and scanned them with her mobile, sending the data to headquarters. Then she bagged them up again and put them in a closet.

She sipped her tea as she messaged with Stoughton. Pella tidied the apartment while keeping an eye on the time and let Lyndon know when it was time to go.

She led her to the same building that housed the Mother Superior's office and brought her to an empty office of her own. "We've got everyone ready to come in and talk to you here; twenty-one people came out to where the body was, so if you want to see them in groups?"

Lyndon nodded. "Except the one who found her first. I'll talk to her separately. First, if she's ready for me."

Pella nodded and left the office. Lyndon realized it was the first time she'd been out of her sight all day, and shook her head in disbelief. The whole experience had been disorienting so far.

As she sat down, it hit her that she didn't have her mobile on her to record or even take notes. Looking through the desk drawers, she found paper and a pen. She tested the ink in a little scribble, then practiced writing her name. It felt foreign; she couldn't remember the last time she'd handwritten anything.

CHAPTER TEN

Pella soon returned, ushering in another young woman in nearly identical garb and with equally long hair, though it was straighter, darker, and loose about her shoulders. She approached the desk with clasped hands and lowered eyes and stood silently.

Pella made eye contact with Lyndon and nodded slightly. "Are you Crystal?" Lyndon asked. The girl nodded without looking up. Lyndon leaned forward, indicating a chair on the other side of the desk. "Have a seat, please," she said. Crystal perched gingerly on the edge of the chair, hands still folded, eyes downcast. "Crystal, I need you to answer my questions as fully as possible, okay? Any little details, anything that occurs to you, no matter how small, feel free to say it. You never know what might help me."

She nodded again. Lyndon suppressed an impatient sigh, wondering how many of the interviewees were going to be postulants. She looked at Pella. "Can you explain to her that I need her to speak freely, and that I won't bite?" she said, in as gentle a tone as she could muster.

Pella hesitated, then put a hand on Crystal's shoulder. When the girl looked up, Pella's hands moved quickly, fingers fluttering in what looked like a pattern or series of signals. Crystal looked doubtful, but Pella kept up the motions until Crystal, with a sidelong glance at Lyndon, moved her own hands almost imperceptibly.

This continued for a few more seconds. Then Crystal lifted her eyes to meet Lyndon's. Pella broke the silence for her. "She didn't mean to be difficult, Miss. She was just waiting to be told to speak."

Lyndon waffled between impatience and pity but kept her expression neutral as she addressed Crystal. "It's okay, I know I'm an outsider and don't do everything the way it's expected here. Can I ask, was that a kind of sign language you were using?"

Finally Crystal spoke in a husky whisper. "Yes, Miss," she said. "We can communicate with each other but we're not allowed to talk, so all the postulants learn it."

"I see," Lyndon said. "And what area are you training in? I understand you all have specialties."

"Yes, Miss. I mostly work in the clinic, learning how to practice medicine."

"So you'll eventually be a doctor or nurse?" Lyndon asked. Crystal nodded with a small smile. "And how long have you been at the convent?"

"Five years."

"So, five more to go before you become a nun?"

Crystal shook her head, and her smile disappeared. "Seven, at least. That's if I don't mess up again."

"That's right; you got another year added the night you found Crenshaw Connelly's body, right?"

This time Crystal shook her head yes. "And I got another one right when I first came here, for trying to whisper to another postulant." She looked off into the distance as she remembered. "I thought if I was quiet enough it wouldn't be detected or something, but I found out it didn't work that way."

"So you went right to eleven years and you stuck with it?" Lyndon asked, a bit incredulously. She nodded again. "Do many postulants make it through the ten years without getting any added on?"

The two girls exchanged glances and smiled ruefully. "Hardly ever," Crystal said. "They usually make a mistake early on. If they're smart, they learn from it and it's just the one. But for lots of us, it happens again."

Lyndon could barely suppress her disgust. The nuns surely knew they'd be getting a dozen years of unpaid servitude out of most postulants, not the ten they advertised. But she wasn't here to try and disrupt the convent's traditions, no matter how unjust they were, so she changed the subject.

"Tell me about the night Ms. Connelly was murdered. Were you already awake or did her screams wake you up?"

"Something woke me up; I didn't know what, so I just lay there. Then I heard footsteps in the hall and ran out to see what was going on."

"How did you find her?"

"It was just luck, Miss. By the time we all got out there it was quiet again, and no one was sure where the sound had come from. So we were just going in all directions, and I happened to come across her."

"And she was on her stomach, and you turned her over?"

"Yes, Miss—I couldn't feel her breathing, and I wanted to see who it was. I figured it wasn't one of us by the clothes, but I couldn't believe my eyes when I saw it was Crenshaw Connelly!"

"You recognized her from TV?"

Crystal nodded excitedly. "We'd all heard she was coming to the resort to film her show. I don't get brought over there very often; usually it's the domestics who do extra work there. But I was hoping I'd somehow get to go while she was there."

"Were you a big fan?"

"Well, I don't know. I only got to see bits and pieces of her show once I got here, but I used to watch it a lot before. I just thought it would be exciting to see someone so famous!" Her face dropped. "I never in a million years thought if I did see her, she'd be on the convent grounds, or—the way she was."

"Dead?" Lyndon prodded gently. Crystal's gaze shifted away; she seemed reluctant to repeat the word or even nod. "Tell me, when you found her, did you notice anything unusual in her scalp or skull?"

Crystal shook her head. "No, Miss. All the wounds looked to be on her back and side. I didn't check under her hair or anything, but I didn't see any blood or anything weird about her hair."

"You work in the clinic; have you seen anyone pass away, or someone who was deceased?"

Another headshake. "It doesn't happen very often here," Crystal finally said after Lyndon waited for a verbal response.

"Where are you from originally?" Lyndon inquired.

Crystal smiled with some pride. "Mars," she said. No wonder she was so enamored of a reality show star, Lyndon thought. She came from a planet ruled by one.

"Did you like it?"

"Oh yes, Miss," Crystal said. "Even though resources are kind of scarce and the climate is pretty harsh, President Gorn has created a beautiful society there."

It was pretty much rote for any Martian to say that about the supposedly benevolent dictator who had taken over Mars when it was a colony of Earth decades before and turned it almost into a cult. Earth audiences were amused and fascinated by his antics on his long-running show, "Dear Leader," and his citizens seemed to uniformly love him, despite troubling reports of poverty, hunger, and health concerns that eclipsed even Earth's many issues.

Crystal continued, interrupting Lyndon's thoughts. "But so have the sisters of Halcyon. It was a hard choice, but I'm—I'll be so happy here." The significance of that self-correction hung in the air for a moment as Lyndon pondered it.

"Anything else you can think of?" she finally asked to break the silence. "Anything at all that comes to mind about that night?"

Crystal hesitated, then signaled another no. "I just feel so bad for her parents," she said. "They must be heartbroken. I wish I could give them some comfort somehow; tell them everything is going to be okay." She shook her head mournfully. "I bet they want to see her so bad. They must miss her."

Lyndon bit back a scoff. It was a nice sentiment, but religious platitudes weren't exactly going to satisfy Connor Connelly. "All right, well, thank you, Crystal, for your time. If you think of anything else, let me know." Even as she said it, she wondered how that would work for someone who felt like she couldn't speak.

CHAPTER ELEVEN

Pella ushered Crystal out and brought in the rest of the witnesses in pairs and threes. The nuns who had been witnesses were easier to get to talk than the postulants, but none of them had any new information. No one had seen even a shadow that might be the assailant leaving the scene. And all claimed to know nothing about the data drive missing from her head.

As the last set of interviewees left the office, Lyndon felt a hollowness in her stomach and realized she'd had nothing to eat since breakfast. As if reading her mind, Pella let her know that dinner was being prepared, and offered to take her to the dining hall.

Lyndon felt weary of the convent's occupants and their odd ways, but she was starving. And besides, the more chances she got to see them, the better her chances of assessing all her potential suspects.

She let Pella lead her through the grounds to yet another building, windows glowing amber with lamplight against the surprisingly early twilight gloom, and into a large hall. The blue-green-swirled white stone walls took on a warmth from the lamps and seemed to dance with other colors, orange and pink and yellow.

In the huge room, at least a hundred nuns were seated around long wooden tables whose legs looked like they were made of thick woody vines intertwined. As Lyndon looked closer, she thought the table legs might be growing out of holes in the floor, like so many things at the convent that looked to be half designed, half part of nature. The dining chairs were covered in the velvety fabric the nuns were fond of using on everything.

Postulants weaved between the tables bearing huge steaming bowls of food and pitchers of water and other liquids. They ladled food and poured drinks, cleaned spills, or stood attentively at the margins of the room waiting to be signaled. There looked to be about two dozen of them.

Lyndon was struck by the youthful beauty of all the women in the huge room. The nuns looked vibrant—like the Mother Superior, their ages were impossible to guess even within a ten-year range—and all the postulants impossibly fresh-faced. Of course no one who could afford otherwise showed their age on Earth, but there was something more genuine about these women's apparent youth.

Pella had paused beside her as she stood just inside the room, taking it all in. "Is this all the nuns?" Lyndon asked quietly.

"No Miss, there are three other dining halls, and they eat in two shifts," Pella replied.

"And where do the postulants eat?"

"The same halls; we also eat in shifts after the nuns are finished, or come get leftovers if we're busy during the regular meal times."

"Do you do this three meals a day?"

"No Miss, just dinner. We mostly have tea for breakfast, and there are breakfast and lunch buffets the nuns can come eat at, or send someone to fetch food from. And us postulants just eat lunch whenever we can fit it in."

Lyndon spotted the Mother Superior around the same time the head nun caught sight of her and beckoned to her. "It looks like the Mother Superior saved you a seat next to her," Pella said, and followed Lyndon closely as she approached the table.

"I'm so glad you could join us. Please, sit down. Pella, serve Officer Bates her dinner." Lyndon thanked her and sat down. The chairs were cushioned and as comfortable as the fabric was soft.

"How did your interviews go?" the nun asked.

"They went fine, ma'am," Lyndon said. "Not much new information, I'm afraid, but everyone was as helpful as they could be."

The Mother Superior nodded. "You'll be wanting to interview the cameraman next, I believe?"

"That's right," Lyndon said. Pella reappeared at her side with a bowl of what looked to be rice covered in a vegetable stew, with a generous slab of rustic bread, slathered in butter. She set it down, unfolded a napkin and laid it in Lyndon's lap, then moved a short distance away.

"Tell me, is Jinx Logan charged with any crimes under Halcyon law?" Lyndon asked.

"No, he's merely being held for questioning about Ms. Connelly's trespassing—and about her murder, of course."

"Have you gotten anything interesting out of him so far?"

"He doesn't seem to know much. He says Ms. Connelly had some sort of jamming device for the sensors that would have set off alarms on their way onto the property, but claims he didn't know she was planning on trespassing until she did it. He tagged along as far as the walls, then waited for her outside it. So technically he didn't trespass himself, although a person wouldn't normally get that close to our walls; the sensors are set several hundred yards away to give us time to respond once the silent alarm is tripped."

"You haven't found the jamming device on the grounds?" The Mother Superior responded in the negative, and Lyndon chewed her food thoughtfully. It was plain but nourishing. The vegetables and spices had much more inherent flavor than most food on Earth, but Lyndon's tastebuds were used to the assertive artificial flavors that were ubiquitous in Earth cuisine.

"Would I be able to question him yet tonight?" Lyndon asked.

"You could, unless you want to wait until tomorrow."

"I'd rather do it tonight, if you don't mind. First thing tomorrow I want to scan the body and send the data back to headquarters for analysis."

"Very well," the Mother Superior said. Pella reappeared with a glass of some fragrant fruit juice and set it down next to Lyndon's food, then backed up a foot or so and hovered behind her chair. Lyndon ate as quickly as she could, trying to act unaware of her attentive gaze.

"That was great, thank you," Lyndon said. "How do I get to where Logan is held?"

"I'll have one of our own peace officers guide you and Pella there."

"Oh, Pella doesn't have to come with me," Lyndon said. "She should stay and have dinner."

"Nonsense," the Mother Superior said, in a manner Lyndon was already familiar with. "She can eat something when she gets back. And she's certainly not going to suffer any ill effects if she skips one meal."

Lyndon restrained herself once again from arguing. *She's here of her own free will,* she reminded herself. If Pella didn't like this treatment, she could always leave.

The Mother Superior sent Pella off with a note, and she soon returned with another nun she introduced as Li. She was dressed the same as the others, but Lyndon recognized the quiet, assessing way she observed everything around her. She was police all right.

Li, Lyndon, and Pella walked together toward the convent gates. Once they were outside them, they walked through grass until they reached the small overhanging open shelter almost like a bus stop, where Lyndon had been dropped off on her way to the convent. Li pushed a button on the wall and within minutes, a driverless car appeared.

The vehicle whisked them along a dark road, illuminated only by the car's headlights. Several minutes later, lights appeared in the distance, and soon the buildings of the resort came into view. Li took it in stride, but when Lyndon glanced over her shoulder at Pella in the back seat, she saw excitement gleaming in her eyes. Lyndon was suddenly glad the Mother Superior had insisted she come.

CHAPTER TWELVE

The streets of the resort looked familiar from videos, but the footage couldn't capture the sense of serenity that the surroundings brought, nor the air's sweetness and the pleasant sounds of water running and tiny birds or insects chirping softly.

There were people out, but it didn't have the frenetic feel of a vacation town where everyone was intent on getting as drunk and rowdy as possible while away from home. People talked and laughed quietly, and most of them wore similar loose-fitting gowns or shorts and shirts that would have looked institutional if they didn't also seem comfortable and luxurious.

The car dropped them outside the most nondescript building on a street, and Li led the way inside. In the lobby area, another nun sat behind a desk, riveted to a large screen on the wall where an episode of "Dear Leader" was playing.

The screen cut from a shot of the round beaming face of President Gorn, a short stocky man who could have been almost any age and race, dressed in an ornate jewel-encrusted jacket, to what looked like a parade of military personnel and vehicles down a thronged street. The sound was turned low, but grandiose marching-band music with an incongruous techno beat could be faintly heard.

The nun tore her eyes away half guiltily and pressed an unseen button under the desk, which enabled Li to open a door into a quiet hallway.

An elevator took them down a couple floors, and they got out in a small jail. Like in most Earth prisons, the cells looked like open cubicles; the doors and the ceilings over each were invisible force fields.

Li took them down the short hallway until they reached the only occupied cell. Inside sat a hunched figure Lyndon remembered from her debriefing: Crenshaw's cameraman, Jinx Logan.

He looked up when they approached, his demeanor wary. He looked even more disheveled than he had in the photo Lyndon had seen.

Lyndon introduced herself and Jinx looked relieved. He stepped as close as the force field would allow. He was eager to explain himself, his words tripping over themselves in his hurry to get them out. He'd thought the trip to the resort would be the sort of travelogue show they'd done dozens of times before.

Like Crenshaw, he had an internal camera, so filming largely meant following her around and looking at her (although there was more skill involved than that). He swore he had no idea Crenshaw had other plans until she dragged him along with her off the resort property.

They'd taken a driverless car part of the way and instructed it to park and wait for them. He described Crenshaw's scrambling app as well as he could and told how she'd had him wait outside. When he heard screams and what sounded like people coming toward the exit, he'd panicked and run back toward the waiting car. But without Crenshaw and her special device, the sensors weren't scrambled; they picked him up as he was leaving, sent out an alarm, and soon led to his capture.

He didn't think the Halcyon officials would have the authority to release him, so he'd held back the footage of that night on the encrypted chip in his camera. Now he opened the file with a few blinks of his eye and a fingertip tap on his temple, and transmitted it to Lyndon's device. She thanked him and assured him she'd review it and send it to headquarters as well.

"If everything's as you say, I'll start the process for having you released," she said. His hangdog expression collapsed a little more at the thought of remaining in prison.

"You won't forget?" he asked. "I really need to get home to Earth; my boyfriend is alone with our baby and I haven't been able to see them or talk to them since this happened."

Lyndon felt a pang of sympathy as well as mild surprise; she hadn't pegged the scruffy guy as a family man. But she reiterated her promise, and they left.

"Could I see a little bit of the resort before we head back?" she asked, mainly for Pella's benefit, and Li relented. The way the postulant's face lit up made Lyndon glad she'd asked.

They strolled down a street paved in cool gray-blue stone, lined with more of the vine-draped trees that seemed to be most common on Halcyon, passing relaxed groups of guests. The occasional car whirred slowly down the street, but compared with cities on Earth, the roads were practically deserted. Others in more fitted clothing that looked like uniforms bustled by occasionally as well.

As they passed one building, from which emanated a fragrance like sweet lavender, Lyndon looked through the open entrance and saw a group of four or five postulants, supervised by a nun, replenishing shelves with slippers, towels, and various toiletries.

Farther down the sidewalk, a uniformed man carrying what looked like a large bag of laundry slowed his hurried pace and then stopped, staring in the trio's direction.

As they drew closer, Lyndon saw that the worker—a good-looking young Black man with shimmering silver accents threaded artfully throughout his black dreadlocks, slender but clearly strong from the casual way he slung the giant bag over his shoulder— wasn't really staring at the group. His eyes were on Pella.

Lyndon watched the two surreptitiously, and kept an eye on Li to see if she noticed. But she'd ignored Pella during the entire expedition and continued to show no interest in her.

The worker shifted to the side to let them pass. He wore a little smile, a dimple appearing in one cheek. Pella kept her head down, but Lyndon saw she too was smiling, and peering up at the young man from the corner of her eye as she walked near him.

They didn't overtly acknowledge one another; no touches or words were exchanged. The moment passed and the trio continued on their way. At the end of the block, Li summoned a car and they drove back toward the convent.

Li parted ways with them as soon as they were back inside the walls, and Pella led Lyndon back to her quarters, though she was starting to feel confident of her bearings herself. She sent the girl away, impatient to start reviewing the footage Jinx had given her.

She opened the file on her mobile device and video started playing in the air in front of her. Crenshaw spoke to the camera as she did much of the time on her show, but her demeanor was radically different from her normal on-air personality. Lyndon felt a chill to see the outfit she'd cut off the body earlier that day, the lifeless face with its grayish cast brought back to stunning vividness.

"I'm nearing the walls of the famed convent of Halcyon," she said as she walked through the grass. Her serious tone was miles from the animated, excitable persona she took on for her show, which everyone thought of as the real Crenshaw Connelly. "Few people not part of the order have ever been inside, and there has never been actual confirmed video footage of the place."

She flicked at a handheld device — activating the alarm scrambler, Lyndon thought — and continued walking, sometimes facing forward, away from the camera, occasionally looking back. Sometimes Jinx's camera moved around and faced her, as if he were walking backward in front of her.

"In a few minutes we'll lose this camera angle, and switch strictly to my POV," she said, pointing at her temple. "Although what I'm doing is strictly forbidden anyway, bringing a man onto the grounds would be tantamount to heresy. So Jinx—" sounding a bit more like her usual self for a moment, familiar enthusiasm rising "—you all know my awesome camera guy Jinx, who's followed me all over the galaxy, helping me chase adventures and capture them for you—Jinx will wait out here while I go look around, and we'll rejoin him when I make my escape." She said the last words with exaggerated drama and a mischievous grin.

Her voice became hushed and serious again, her words sounding like a script she'd written and memorized. "The sisters of Halcyon have been the subject of many rumors—about what it looks like inside these walls, about their rituals and traditions, about strange powers or abilities—and this is my first attempt to penetrate their walls and find some answers."

After more dramatic build-up—Crenshaw seemed to be going for a completely different feel in this footage, but she couldn't resist the time-padding blathering that both enraged people and kept them glued to her show—she finally went to the wall. She slowly climbed its sheer face, clearly getting some kind of technology assist. Lyndon made a note to study the garments more closely, and wondered if the analysis of the scans she'd sent to headquarters would turn up a sophisticated rock-climbing mechanism built right into the clothes.

Once Crenshaw had gone over the wall, the footage ended. Jinx had evidently stopped filming while waiting and been too panicked to film any part of his attempt to flee after hearing screams.

Lyndon sent a copy of the video to headquarters. Not even slightly sleepy, she left her apartment and walked out into the courtyard, then through the archway to the larger grounds. The air was cool and sweet and flooded with moonlight. Lyndon marveled at the large, pristine white orb in the sky, feeling for the first time that she was on an alien world. *In an alien body,* she thought.

She strolled further, relishing her solitude. No one else was out except a few unfamiliar nocturnal creatures she spied scurrying or flying around in the dark, and all the buildings were dark. There were no lights on the grounds, but the moon provided ample light to see where she was going.

She wandered down a gentle slope, taking careful note of her route so she'd be able to find her way back to her quarters.

She passed the small pool she'd been given a drink of water from, and the rock that she knew housed the tunnel to the food storage cave and de facto morgue.

Down another slope she saw a larger pond, shimmering in a way that seemed like it contained its own illumination, not just borrowed moonlight. And realized she wasn't the only person out in the middle of the night after all.

CHAPTER THIRTEEN

A small group of nuns and postulants—three of each, Lyndon was able to discern by their outfits as she drew closer—encircled an oblong shape by the water's edge.

A faint, rhythmic murmur, like a recited prayer, floated on the air to Lyndon's ear, but she couldn't even make it out enough to know whether it was in English or another language.

Lyndon saw a promising hiding spot closer to the pond in a trio of trees with plenty of leafy cover dripping from their branches, so she dropped to her stomach and crawled cautiously toward it. The group at the pond seemed intent on the object they were gathered around, but she didn't want to take any chances.

Ensconced safely in the shadows, she knelt up and peered between the vines. She could see and hear more and even recognized the faces of a couple of the nuns from the dinner hall earlier. The words they were chanting weren't in English. The object of their rapt attention, Lyndon saw, was a rectangular shape, about six feet by three and two feet high, draped with a silky white cloth that covered it completely.

The women stretched out their hands over it, and their voices grew louder. They raised their arms slowly, and Lyndon watched in disbelief as the object appeared to follow, lifting gradually into the air. The movement was so imperceptible that Lyndon thought she was imagining it until she noted that the edges of the cloth no longer touched the ground.

The object continued its gradual ascent until it hovered about three feet off the ground, suspended seemingly without supports below it or ropes or wires holding it from above.

The women facing away from the pond began to swivel toward it, backing up slowly, not lowering their arms. Once there was a clear space, the thing began moving horizontally into the space over the pond. Soon all six women were lined up shoulder to shoulder, arms out, still chanting.

Once it had reached the approximate center of the pond, the object stopped. Three of the women kept their arms outstretched; the other three lowered theirs, then raised them again, this time slowly extending them higher than chest level, stretching them out as if offering something to the pond, though their hands looked to be empty.

Watching this movement, Lyndon at first missed what was happening on the surface of the pond. A change in the light caught her attention.

Below the cloth-covered object, the water was stirring. Lyndon wouldn't have known what to call the movement; it wasn't waves exactly, and the disturbances were localized under the object. The rest of the pond's surface remained placid.

The ripples that formed remained, instead of constantly shifting like natural water movement. They grew into a curved ridge that mirrored the rectangular shape of the thing that hovered above it.

Misty sprays of water began emanating from the liquid ridge, going higher and higher until they were cascading onto the cloth. But somehow, as far as Lyndon could tell, the cloth wasn't getting drenched as she expected. It sparkled, perhaps with droplets of water, or with something else entirely.

The object began to glow, growing gradually brighter. One of the women cried out in surprise or fear, but the chanting continued.

Slowly the glowing thing began moving, following the same path back toward the group. The six women parted ranks slowly, eyes glued to it, arms still outstretched, and once again surrounded the object.

As Lyndon watched in disbelief, the cloth on top stirred and moved, and something swelled or rose against it on one end. The shape moved upward until it resembled a human figure, shrouded in the shimmering white fabric, standing in the object, which now appeared to be a coffin-shaped box.

The chanting died away uncertainly, not on a definite note but gradually as each woman fell into a hushed silence one by one, lowering their arms and standing frozen.

Then the figure began to make its own noise, a strange inhuman sound that started low and guttural and rose to a keening wail. The cloth moved and one end of it lifted up, as if the thing had arms that it was stretching out as the nuns and postulants had done earlier. One of the girls in postulant clothes stumbled backward and almost fell, but managed to catch herself.

The shrouded creature moaned and the group around it remained rooted in place for a few seconds that felt like an eternity to Lyndon. At last, one of the nuns moved toward the box and reached out to take what must have been the hands of the figure. It grasped wildly at the nun's hands through the fabric, and in its frenzy fell forward and nearly toppled out of the compartment.

The other two nuns rushed forward and gripped the figure on each side, supporting it, while the three postulants hung back, whether in awe or terror Lyndon couldn't be sure. As the nuns held on to the thing, it falteringly stepped out onto the white rock on which the box rested.

It swayed and staggered, and two of the nuns took one another's hands behind the figure and gently nudged it into a sitting position on their linked arms. Their other clasped hands supported its back.

The glow was starting to fade, but it still illuminated the nuns' faces as they turned to ascend the gentle slope in Lyndon's direction.

CHAPTER FOURTEEN

Startled into action, Lyndon flattened herself onto the ground and crept farther back into the trees.

The third nun and the three postulants each picked up a corner of the box, which seemed light judging by the easy way they lifted it, and followed the three nuns carrying the figure, now slumped in their arms as if unconscious.

Lyndon strained to duck down even farther, though she was about as close to the ground as she could realistically go. The two small groups came within about twenty feet of her as they wound their way past her hiding place up the hill. As they passed, Lyndon studied their faces, trying to memorize them. Two of the nuns she'd seen before and would recognize easily if she saw them again, so she concentrated on the others.

The postulant facing away from her looked around, and the moonlight picked out her features in perfect clarity: Crystal. Her face looked solemn and frightened, much more so even than it had been during Lyndon's interview with her.

None of the women spared even a glance at the stand of trees, luckily, and moved slowly away until they were out of sight. Lyndon lay a while longer until they were long gone. Then she got to her feet and made her way cautiously back to her apartment, hugging the shadows, trees, and walls as she did.

She got back without encountering anyone and unlocked her door with the old-fashioned key. Kicking off her boots, she collapsed on the bed, but as exhausted as she felt, sleep did not come to her that night until dawn began to glow behind her curtains.

* * *

She slept hard in the short time she had and was disoriented when a faint sound woke her up. She realized it was a light tapping on her door. She dragged herself up, still fully clothed, and stumbled to the door.

Pella stood outside, dressed in a coarse fabric dress virtually identical to the one she'd worn the day before … had it been only one day that Lyndon had known her? It seemed longer somehow. "I came to see if you'd like me to bring you some breakfast, Miss, or if you'd rather go to the dining hall."

Lyndon considered the options. She wanted to see the members of the group she'd spied on last night but also wondered what information she might be able to get out of Pella.

"I'd rather eat here, but only if you'll bring something for yourself and have breakfast with me. Okay?"

Pella hesitated, then nodded. "Okay. Thank you, Miss."

She returned about fifteen minutes later with a large covered platter. She put on water to boil for tea and prepared two plates of food, then took a small wooden folding table out of one of the closets and set it next to the armchair Lyndon was sitting in. She set one plate and cup of tea on it, then sat cross-legged on the floor with hers.

"Thank you," Lyndon said. The girl nodded and smiled, her wavy blond hair picking up glints of sunlight. Lyndon tried not to notice the way her dress had hiked up when she sat down, or how soft and inviting her full thighs looked. Her attraction to women hadn't stayed behind with her male body, she reflected, then stopped herself from going any farther with that train of thought.

Lyndon forced herself to focus on her food instead. She picked up a slab of dark bread slathered with a thick, rich, savory spread, somewhere between butter and hummus. She took a bite; she couldn't place the flavor but it was rich and hearty and somehow perfect for breakfast. The plate also contained a pile of chopped mixed fruit that resembled but wasn't quite like anything she'd had on Earth. She sampled each type separately, caught up in the unfamiliar but appealing flavors, some tart and some sweet. "We don't get anything like this on Earth anymore," she told Pella.

"I know," Pella said. "When I first got here I couldn't believe it either." She popped a piece of fruit in her mouth and chewed with satisfaction.

"You're from Earth originally?"

Pella nodded and swallowed the fruit. "Most of us are. The order started there. That was a long time ago, but we still have lots of supporters on Earth."

Lyndon studied another piece of foreign fruit. "In some ways I can see why you'd want to join. The air, the food, plants; everything's so much healthier here. But this ten-year postulant thing seems really harsh. I guess if you're a believer it's worth it."

Pella shrugged. "That's part of it. But it's also about what we had on Earth. A lot of us didn't have much of a chance for a good life there. You know how it is, right, Miss?"

Lyndon assented uncomfortably. It hadn't even been a question as an upper middle-class teenage boy whether getting into and affording whatever college Lyndon was interested in would be possible. It was a given. In fact, though the National Police Force had one of the most elite and prestigious military academies on Earth, his parents had viewed it as somewhat of a step down when he'd chosen to attend it.

Lyndon knew most Earth inhabitants wouldn't go to college, wouldn't be able to pay back student loan debts if they did, wouldn't be able to move up the career or social ladder. He knew he occupied a position of privilege.

Pella nodded knowingly. "Well, at the end of this, if I get through it, is a pretty comfortable life, on a planet that's in much better shape than Earth. And even if this part is hard, in a lot of ways it's easier than my life might've ended up there." She smiled a bit wryly. "So, you know, you don't have to feel too sorry for me. And I know I can leave anytime. But seeing what most people in my family went through on Earth, I really don't want to go back to that. I want security." She bit her lip and her expression clouded over. "I just hope ..."

"What?"

Pella shook her head. "It's nothing. I—well, when the sisters started sending us to the resort to work more, that was a big change. It's been fun, but it did make me wonder. And some of the other girls are a little worried that the convent isn't—doing so well, you know, in terms of money." She hesitated. "I thought they were making too much of it, but then, one night—"

She leaned forward and her voice became quieter, almost a whisper. "I was dusting in the Mother Superior's library, and she was in her office, which is right next to it. The door between them was open. She was talking to somebody on her computer, and she sounded angry. She doesn't really lose her temper, like, ever."

"Did you hear what she was mad about?" Lyndon asked.

"Well, I couldn't hear the person on the other side of it, so it was hard to figure out exactly what she was talking about. But she said stuff like, 'I know what you're trying to do and it won't work.' Or another time she said 'The convent will survive. It'll always survive.' And then something like 'You're not getting this planet from us.'"

CHAPTER FIFTEEN

Lyndon tried to disguise her excitement. "When was this?"

"A month or so ago, I think. Maybe it was more recent. I have a hard time keeping track."

"Have you heard anything like that since then?"

Pella shook her head. "Just rumors from some of the other postulants, but I don't think they know anything either."

Lyndon pondered as they ate the rest of their breakfast in silence. Pella gathered their plates and took them to the kitchen, pouring

Lyndon another cup of the strong, dark tea. She brought it to her, looking worried.

"Please Miss, you won't tell the Mother Superior, will you? That I overheard her, and that I told you?"

"Of course not," Lyndon said. "And thank you for telling me. Even though it probably has nothing to do with the murder, you never know what might end up being useful. If you find out anything else that seems at all out of the ordinary—"

Pella assented. "I'll tell you right away, Miss," she said.

"And if you could put in a good word for me with the other postulants, like you did with Crystal ..." Lyndon said. "Please tell them they can come to me with anything unusual, no matter how small."

* * *

Lyndon sent Pella to find the Mother Superior and arrange for another visit to the de facto morgue, this time with her mobile device to do a full scan and analysis of the corpse. While the girl was gone, Lyndon got in touch with Stoughton.

"Had you heard anything about the convent being in financial trouble, sir?" she asked the Commander. "Do they have shareholders or debt to anyone?"

She saw him shake his head on the screen projected in front of her. "I'll have someone do some digging down here. We hadn't really looked into that because by all accounts, the resort brings in a reliable income, plus more than one wealthy benefactor has left them the majority of their estate. And they've still got supporters who send them money."

"Plus, having met the Mother Superior, it's hard to imagine her letting anyone have a stake in the planet or wanting to be in debt," Lyndon offered. "She likes being in control. But what I heard from the source"—she'd decided to keep Pella a confidential informant for now—"made it sound like someone thought they could take over the planet. Buy it out from under the convent maybe?"

Stoughton's brow wrinkled. "Bet there's only a handful of people in our galaxy rich enough to even put a down payment on a planet like that."

"Well, maybe make some inquiries. But keep it pretty subtle, if you could, sir; I don't want to raise alarm bells until we learn more." Lyndon paused. "Connor Connelly—is he one of them?"

"One of who?"

"People rich enough to buy Halcyon if it was for sale?"

Stoughton nodded reluctantly. He'd clearly taken a shine to Connelly, possibly enjoying having a close association with someone so massively rich and famous.

"Seems like it could be more than a coincidence that his daughter was sneaking around the grounds and wound up dead," Lyndon said. She heard a light tap on her door. "Speaking of, I've got to go take another look at her body now, sir. I'll update you on a few other things that've happened and send the body scan when I get back to my room."

She ended the connection with Stoughton and opened the door to Pella. The girl bobbed her head. "The Mother Superior says we can go over to the caves now, Miss. She'll meet us there."

* * *

It had turned into a cloudy, misty day, but somehow it was even more beautiful, not depressing and dirty-looking like a rainy day on Earth.

Pella had brought an old-fashioned umbrella—Lyndon still found herself surprised and amused by all the things in active use at the convent that she'd only ever seen in movies and museums—and offered to hold it over her. She declined, enjoying the fresh feeling of the droplets landing gently on her skin as they walked the now familiar route to the door in the rock.

The Mother Superior had just arrived and greeted Lyndon while Pella got the door open and lit the lantern as she had last time. They traversed the downward-sloping hallway together. Lyndon's mind was full to bursting with memories of the ceremony she'd witnessed, which she didn't want to talk about with the Mother Superior. Pella, of course, had lapsed into silence now that they were in someone else's company. The Mother Superior herself said little, other than inquiring if she'd slept well and whether Pella was being a good girl, both of which Lyndon confirmed, though she wondered if her face reflected her lack of sleep.

After what seemed like an eternity of awkward exchanges and long pauses, they at least reached the chamber. Pella went around lighting the wall lanterns while the Mother Superior approached a large oblong wooden box in the corner.

"Pella should be able to help you move the body back to the table," she said, "but if you want me to summon others to help you, don't hesitate to ask." She clearly had no interest in handling a cadaver herself. It wasn't a question of having the strength; she easily lifted the heavy top off the box by herself and set it on the floor, then stood by.

Lyndon and Pella approached the box, Pella with visible reluctance. Lyndon looked in to assess the best way to handle the body, then bent closer to examine the container's interior.

There was a rumpled pile of cloth that didn't look like it covered anything. Lyndon reached in and lifted it out, having to grab several handfuls to pull the entire voluminous piece of material out, and saw with disbelief the bottom of the box. Empty.

CHAPTER SIXTEEN

Lyndon looked up from the box and fixed the Mother Superior with a hard glare. "Where is it?"

In the ensuing rush of exclamations of surprise and protestations of ignorance, Pella backed away against a wall, eyes wide and confused. The Mother Superior spotted her and sent her to fetch law enforcement.

While they waited for police to arrive, Lyndon and the Mother Superior searched every container, shadowy corner and any other possible hiding place, but there was no sign of Crenshaw's corpse. Pella returned with Li and two other nuns, who examined the box and repeated the search of the premises.

Meanwhile, Lyndon and the Mother Superior, who was uncharacteristically rattled, spoke in a corner in low heated tones.

"Who has access to this place?"

"Well, everyone. It's just a storage room, not a vault."

Lyndon swore under her breath. "So anyone could've taken her. Well, it's not ideal to have a search party made up of suspects, but that's the situation we have here. I'm going to need as many people as you can spare to comb the grounds, starting here and working out in all directions. I know you don't have security cameras guarding the perimeter; is there any way to tell if there was a signal disruption to your alarm, similar to what Crenshaw did when she broke in here?"

The Mother Superior nodded, looking like she was biting back an argument. Probably not used to anyone taking a sharp tone with her, Lyndon thought, but she didn't have the luxury of playing nice anymore.

The law enforcement officials had
completed their search by then. "Are there any
other entrances to this room besides the one we
came through?" Lyndon asked. They answered
in the negative. "Good. I want one of you to
stand guard at the cave entrance and make
sure no one else comes in here. The rest of you,
gather whoever can join the search party."

"Why do we need to guard this place?" the
Mother Superior asked sharply, as if to try and
regain authority. "We've searched it twice. The
body's not here."

"There may be evidence, ma'am," Lyndon
said, irritated. "As soon as I've got the search
started I'm going to come back in here and do a
scan. Ideally I'd have a forensics specialist here,
but I'll have to do the best I can."

Once she had one of the nuns stationed at
the rock entrance, Li hurried to a nearby
building with a belfry and rang out a call.
Nuns and postulants emerged from buildings
and appeared from other parts of the grounds,
gathering in a loose crowd around Li, who had

climbed on a boulder in the middle of the clearing.

She explained what had happened, and despite her businesslike tone, there were gasps and murmurs from the assembled nuns. Lyndon heard at least one ominous beep that suggested an unfortunate postulant in the crowd had forgotten herself and joined the chorus.

Under the direction of Li, the Mother Superior, and several other nuns in the law enforcement department, the women were divided into groups of three or four and sent off in all directions. Lyndon spotted Crystal about to go off in a quartet and hurried to stop her. "Could I talk to you for a few minutes?"

Crystal looked surprised but nodded, glancing at the Mother Superior as if for confirmation. The nun also nodded, but there was a puzzled crease in her forehead. "I want to go over the events of the night Ms. Connelly was murdered one more time," Lyndon lied, sensing that either the Mother Superior didn't know Crystal had been out the night before and Crystal didn't want her to know, or that she *did* know and was concerned Lyndon knew something about it and was going to ask questions about secret ceremonies. She didn't want the Mother Superior hovering in either case.

"Ma'am, I'm just going to take a walk with Crystal. I'll be back to scan the cave and check on the progress of the search party in a little while." She looked at Li. "Will you ring the bell if someone finds the body, or any evidence of where it went?"

Li nodded. "I'll do a single chime if that happens."

"Good," Lyndon said. "Come with me, Crystal, please."

The postulant tagged along as Lyndon walked briskly away, outpacing the slow-moving search parties who were scrutinizing the ground and foliage as they went.

Lyndon waited until they were well out of earshot of anyone else before speaking. "Please answer all my questions as thoroughly as possible," she said, feeling a sense of deja vu from the last time she'd spoken to the girl.

Crystal nodded.

"Where were you last night?" The girl's eyes widened in surprise. "We don't know when the body may have been moved. Were you anywhere on the grounds where you may have seen something?"

Crystal's mouth hung open as she struggled to find words. Lyndon wondered if the collar around her neck served as a lie detector too; would it count as disobedience if she answered less than truthfully?

"I—I didn't see her body get moved from the cave," she answered at last. Her breath caught and Lyndon surmised she was listening for a beep. *Good,* she thought grimly. It probably would detect lies, and the look on her face suggested she'd given an evasive answer that wasn't a lie but concealed something.

"Were you out of your dorm after dark?" Lyndon pressed.

"Yes," Crystal said reluctantly.

"When did you leave your room? How long were you out? Did you return to the dorm later?"

Crystal squirmed. Lyndon stopped walking so she could focus more fully on the girl's face. "I left a little before midnight, and I got back to my room probably around two or two-thirty. I don't know the exact time."

"That's fine," Lyndon said. "Were you with anyone during that time?"

"Yes," Crystal said miserably.

"Who?"

"Three of the sisters and two other postulants."

"No one else was there?"

Crystal hesitated. "No?" As she waited tensely, her collar emitted a long beep, strident in the silence. The tracker lit up with a number 7, which flickered and changed to an 8. The postulant let out a sound like a strangled sob.

CHAPTER SEVENTEEN

Lyndon smiled grimly, feeling very little pity in her anger at Crenshaw's disappearance. "I'll take that as a yes, Crystal, and it seems you have to answer me truthfully from now on if you don't want more years added." Tears welled up in Crystal's eyes. "Now, describe your activities last night. What were you doing?"

"I—I—" Crystal bit her lip. "It was a religious rite, Miss. I was helping the nuns with a ceremony."

"And did it have to do with this seventh person you tried to tell me wasn't there?"

"Yes, Miss," Crystal mumbled.

"So who exactly was this person? A nun or a postulant? And what was the ritual about?"

Crystal looked at her in horrified silence.

"Answer me!" Lyndon commanded.

The girl remained mute. After several seconds of withering under Lyndon's glare, her face collapsed in grief as her tracker beeped again. The 8 appeared and flashed to 9. She mouthed a word: "Please."

"What is it?" Lyndon asked.

Crystal fell to her knees, bending down so her forehead touched Lyndon's boots. "Please don't ask me about the ritual, Miss! I'll do anything. We're never supposed to reveal our rites to outsiders. I could be cast out forever."

"And what if you keep refusing to answer me and you keep getting years added?" Lyndon demanded in a callous tone, but her stomach was starting to churn. "You'll be a slave forever."

Crystal didn't or couldn't respond. She prostrated herself on the ground, clutching one of Lyndon's ankles, her body wracked with sobs.

Lyndon looked down at the trembling girl, shaking her head. She swore softly. "All right, get up," she said, trying to maintain a cold tone.

Crystal slowly stood, her eyes red and her nose runny. She lifted her dress a few inches by the neckline and wiped her face on the inside of it, then dropped her hands by her side and stood with her head bowed, clearly trying to regain control of her body, though it still shook with suppressed sobs.

Lyndon felt a sickening pang of guilt, thinking about the two years she'd added to the girl's servitude. But then she thought of Crenshaw's tragically lifeless body—and of her own career being potentially ruined if she didn't find it—and it receded. "Tell me one more thing and I'll let you go. Does the Mother Superior know about the ceremony you performed last night?"

Crystal sniffed, then shook her head slowly. Lyndon waited for a beep, but none came. "All right. I won't tell her—for now. Go to your room. Clean up and calm down, then join one of the search parties."

Crystal nodded without looking directly at Lyndon and hurried off, her shoulders hunched in a piteous attitude of defeat.

* * *

The fruitless search continued through the afternoon. Lyndon scanned the cave and the entire tunnel leading to it with her mobile and retreated to her quarters to send the data to headquarters for analysis. Then, filled with dread, called Stoughton.

The Commander was predictably furious. "You had no goddamn security around that body?"

"I'm sorry, sir," Lyndon said glumly. "It was hugely careless of me to assume the body would be safe there." She bit back further explanation about her disorientation in her new body, on a new planet with strange new rules and customs, that would've sounded like she was trying to make excuses.

Stoughton swore for what seemed like five minutes, then attempted to get his anger under control. "All right, so what now?"

"I sent the scan of the cave where the body was stored. I doubt there'll be anything of use, but see what you can get from it. Since anyone could access the place, DNA won't necessarily tell us anything."

Stoughton sighed heavily. "And we'll continue searching the grounds," Lyndon added. "Also, depending on when the body was taken, I'm almost positive someone saw something."

She told Stoughton about the weird ritual and Crystal's refusal to explain it. "The nuns of Halcyon are known for staying youthful. I'm sure it was some sort of rejuvenation ceremony. But for some reason it was a secret from the Mother Superior, so I'm going to have trouble getting anyone to talk."

"Why don't you tell the bitch? Not your secret to keep."

Lyndon hesitated. "I don't know, sir, but I have a hunch I can get more mileage out of what I saw if I keep it from the Mother Superior for a while. Makes the others feel like I'm on their side."

Stoughton shrugged. "Go with it, then. But try to find out who else was at that ceremony and question them."

"Will do, sir," Lyndon said, relieved that Stoughton still somewhat trusted her judgment after the missing body fiasco. "Did you find anything out about the convent's financial situation?"

Stoughton's face fell a little. "Nothing about them facing any financial difficulty. But I did some digging and—" his voice lowered, although he seemed to be in the room alone "—it turns out Connor Connelly had some interest in buying Halcyon."

"Really?"

"Yeah, made an offer on it about five years ago. Nothing since then, so it's hard to think it's related to this shit show."

Yeah, but not impossible, whether you like it or not, Lyndon thought grimly. "Well, let me know if anything comes of that lead," she said, hoping to subtly drive home the point that it shouldn't be dropped just to do the Commander's new friend a favor.

Stoughton nodded reluctantly. "Back to it, officer. Keep me posted."

"Yes sir."

"Oh, and Bates? That cameraman can be released. I want you to go to the resort and personally escort him from the holding cell to the transport station. Have him sent to us for routine questioning."

Lyndon felt impatient; there was so much to be done still at the convent. But she knew she was the only Earth law enforcement officer on Halcyon, so she simply agreed.

* * *

The clouds had cleared and a colorful sunset cast a rosy glow over everything as the driverless car carried Lyndon to the streets of the resort, stopping in front of the police station. Lyndon entered and told the nun at the lobby desk what she was there to do.

The nun nodded. "Yes ma'am, your headquarters contacted us. We're checking him out now; we just need to do a health scan and exit interview for our records." She indicated a nearby bench. "It'll be a few minutes; we'll bring him out when we're done."

Lyndon sat and leaned back against the wall. Her eyes went to the TV, realizing how quickly unusual it had become to have a show on, and how little she'd missed it. On Earth you could hardly be anywhere without a show playing on a holoscreen somewhere.

A promo for a show was playing, frenetic music pounding and quick cuts flashing across the screen. "The search is on," a dramatic voice-over exclaimed, as snippets of various beautiful and outlandishly dressed people appeared one after another in rapid succession. "The search for an unforgettable look. A towering talent. An over-the-top personality."

The snippets sped up into a blur until they ended with an empty room. The voice-over said the words as they slammed onto the screen accompanied by dramatic synth beats: "Who's Living la Vida Next?"

CHAPTER EIGHTEEN

Lyndon's mouth dropped open. She didn't have any illusions that Connor Connelly was a tasteful individual, but putting on a reality contest to replace your dead daughter in a long-running reality show that had never been about anyone but her? That was trashy even for him. If he was callous enough to do that, was he heartless enough to have her killed in order to create a publicity crisis and ruin the nuns, forcing them to sell?

The promo over, the TV cut to the opening credits of "Dear Leader." "I'm President Gorn," said the diminutive round-faced star of the show, accompanied by quirky music. "But the people of Mars call me 'Dear Leader.' You're about to see just another day in my life."

Typically the next part of the show was a montage of things to come, snippets of the wild antics and over-the-top luxuries of the leader. But this episode started differently, with a shot of Gorn seated on a ridiculously bejeweled throne that dwarfed his already short frame. Despite the comically tacky set, his face was uncharacteristically solemn.

"My friends, I'm coming to you with a message of vital importance about a disease that has infected our galaxy," he intoned, tenting his ring-laden fingers under his chin.

"My dear friend and the producer of this show—as well as the owner of this entire network—recently lost not only his second-biggest star after me, but his beloved daughter, the light of his life."

Lyndon scoffed inwardly; the melodramatic words seemed even more empty in light of the promo she'd just seen.

"Now, you've all heard about poor, lovely Crenshaw's death, but no details, right? Just lots of rumors. Well, I've heard the same rumors, but I've also heard from a credible source what really happened on Halcyon." Gorn leaned forward confidingly. "It pains me to the very core of my being to share with you, dear viewers, that our 'La Vida' darling was brutally, cruelly … murdered."

Low, menacing music came up. "You've all heard about Halcyon. If you somehow hadn't before, you saw it on sweet Crenshaw's final episodes of 'La Vida.' A spa planet, run by nuns—sounds harmless, huh? Sure, we don't know anything about them, but what could be bad about a group of ladies who like to pray a lot?" The music continued to grow in volume and drama. "Why don't we ask someone who used to live on Halcyon? But she wasn't a nun."

The screen cut to a darkened room, where the silhouette of a woman's head could be faintly seen. Gorn's voice continued its narration. "Before a nun becomes a nun on

Halcyon, she has to spend time being what's called a postulant. This beautiful young lady — we'll call her Cat — spent eight years of her life as a postulant. Eight years! Do you think she qualified to be a nun after that? No! Girls have to be postulants for a minimum of ten years, and often it's much longer. Cat will explain that in a moment.

"So you're asking yourself, 'What's a postulant, anyway? A nun in training? What does it matter how long it takes, when you get to be where you want to be either way?' Let's let Cat tell you."

He went silent and the girl began to speak. Her voice was obviously altered to disguise its true sound. It was higher-pitched than a normal voice and slightly distorted.

"I joined the convent to have a better life. The nuns were so nice during the interview. They explained the basic rules, about postulants being like the maids of the convent, but I didn't know what it would be like until I started there." Her voice choked up.

"I wasn't a maid, I was a slave," she said. "I had no rights. We weren't even allowed to speak unless a nun told us to. We worked from sunup to sundown, getting ordered around constantly."

"Sounds horrible," Gorn's voice piped up. "So what happened to postulants who failed to obey? Were they beaten? Starved? No, it was actually much worse."

He fell silent and Cat began to talk again. "Every postulant got this thing put around her neck that counted down the ten years. Well, if you made even a tiny mistake, the tracker could tell, and it would add a whole year." The dim outline shook her head. "I forgot to do one chore out of hundreds one day, and I got a year added. I accidentally said 'thank you' to another postulant who helped me with something, and boom. Another year. At the end of eight years, I still had another six years to go! I couldn't do it anymore."

Gorn's voice-over broke in again. "One of the rules is that postulants can leave whenever they want. So, it's not that bad, right? The convent even pays them for their time and helps them get a job somewhere. Pretty great deal?"

As if in response, Cat said, "The Mother Superior had said they'd help me out if I left the convent, pay me for the time I'd worked. But when I chose to leave, they gave me barely enough actual money for fare back to Earth. They kept most of it—said it was to cover room and board over the years. I was homeless and had nothing to eat. I ended up turning tricks to try and make enough to survive." Her voice choked up. "There was no help finding a job. They wouldn't even respond to messages I tried to send."

Her hand came up as if wiping tears from the corners of her eyes. "I wasted eight years of my life working my ass off to serve these nuns, and they just cut me off!"

Gorn was back on screen in his gaudily opulent throne. "So before you say that a nun is too harmless to murder another human being, please consider what else these nuns are capable of. We'll have more after these messages." The ominous music swelled to a climax, the name of the show flashed on screen, and commercials came on.

Lyndon had been riveted to the screen, but now she looked at the desk. The nun behind it had risen to her feet and was also staring at the screen, horror-stricken.

As if on cue, a door opened and Jinx came out, accompanied by two more nuns.

Jinx saw Lyndon and broke into a grateful grin. "You remembered! Oh man, my boyfriend's going to be so relieved. Hey, can I get my mobile back so I can message him?" He looked between Lyndon and the nun behind the desk, noticing their shocked expressions. "What's wrong?"

CHAPTER NINETEEN

The nun quickly recovered some surface composure. She brought out a soft cloth bag and handed it hastily to Jinx. "We're done here. Here's all your belongings. Officer, you can take him to the transport station now."

Lyndon wanted to stay and see what she told the other two nuns—who looked cheerfully unaware of what had just aired on galactic television—and what other revelations came next on the show. But the first nun stared pointedly at her, saying nothing, and she gave in. "All right, come on, Logan. There's just a little more red tape and then you'll be a free man."

Even before the door closed behind them Lyndon could hear the frantic whispering begin.

* * *

The mood that night, when Pella knocked at Lyndon's apartment door to bring her to dinner, was somber and subdued. Word had obviously gotten around of President Gorn's bombshell exposé.

Lyndon had watched the rest of the episode and there was nothing informative, just vague rumors and footage of nuns and postulants filmed at the resort, slowed down and darkened to make everything seem menacing. But it didn't change the explosive nature of that first segment.

As they walked to the dining hall, Lyndon asked Pella whether she'd heard about it. "Yes Miss, right before I left the dorm to come get you. My friend Marci overheard a couple of the nuns talking about it and told a bunch of us."

"What did you think?" Lyndon asked.

Pella wrinkled her nose. "I don't believe it, but it worries me."

"What don't you believe?"

"Well, the part about getting cheated when she left, not being given a fair amount of money."

"But all the other parts were accurate, or seemed like they could be true, right?"

"Well, yes, but she made it sound like everything's designed to be mean, or cheat us."

"You don't think that?"

Pella shook her head emphatically. "I mean, it's a trade-off. You know how it's going to be and you can choose not to do it. The Mother Superior doesn't make out like it's easy when you join."

Lyndon thought. "If you don't believe her, why are you worried?"

"It's talking about things most people didn't know about our order. It sounds worse than it is, so it might turn people against us. You know, donors, and people coming to the spa." She shivered. "If we're having money trouble already, that show could hurt us even more."

Lyndon suddenly remembered that Crystal was a former citizen of Mars. "Was Crystal there when you found out?"

"I don't think so," Pella said hesitantly. "If she wasn't, she'll know by now. Everyone's talking about it."

Despite what Pella said, no one spoke directly about the show during dinner, and Lyndon refrained from asking the Mother Superior about it in such a public space. Her response would be so tempered by wanting to save face as to be useless, Lyndon thought.

She did ask her about the security system and learned there had been no disruption to it that day. So no one had left the convent grounds unauthorized or unidentified. *Unless they had something more sophisticated than Crenshaw's signal jammer,* Lyndon's brain warned her.

The search parties had made it through the entire convent grounds, wall to wall, with no sign of the body. Maybe it had been buried or hidden somewhere on the grounds, but there were no clues as to where, how and by whom.

Lyndon would have another search party spread out through the area outside the convent walls the next day, but she didn't mention it to the Mother Superior where everyone else could hear. If one of the women present had used the alarm blocker to leave and come back in undetected, she didn't want them to know she'd considered that possibility.

Pella accompanied Lyndon back to her room, although she knew the way by now. She went through her habitual tidying and tea-making, while Lyndon rewatched the "Dear Leader" episode. The entire thing was designed to cast a suspicious light on the Sisters of Halcyon. "Cat" was well-disguised; it was impossible to make out any details of her face or hair, and her accent was nondescript.

Whoever she was, Lyndon wondered, could she have a motive for murdering Crenshaw or be in league with someone still in the convent who did? Perhaps she'd wanted to bring scrutiny to the order.

Lyndon wondered if the Mother Superior knew who the girl was. Another thing to discuss with her in the morning. How many postulants had ever left the order and how recently had someone defected? That could narrow the field considerably, assuming the girl was at least partly telling the truth and not a complete fraud hired by Gorn to lie. But if she was, how did she get so many details of Halcyon culture right? And why would he do that?

Lyndon started to replay it, but just at that moment Pella brought her tea, so she paused it and put down her mobile. As the postulant leaned over to set it on a small table beside her chair, her full breast, encased in but seemingly loose under the coarse garment she wore, brushed against Lyndon's arm.

It caught her by surprise and she hissed involuntarily with a sharp intake of breath. Pella had never touched her before, even accidentally. Something about the way the girl didn't move away quickly gave Lyndon pause. When she did back away, it was only slightly, and a small smile hovered about her lips, tentative but knowing.

"Would you like me to give you a massage, Miss?" she asked, her voice soft. "I've received training in that here."

Lyndon hesitated, confused thoughts flooding through her mind. Although she'd noticed Pella's body from the first moment she saw her, she'd successfully compartmentalized that admiration and kept it at bay in light of her assignment, the rules of the convent, and the uneven power dynamic between them. If she started being touched by Pella, even in a clinical way, it might start to erode the wall behind which she'd put her attraction to the postulant.

"That's thoughtful of you to offer, Pella, but I think I'm fine."

"Please forgive me if I'm overstepping my bounds, Miss, but you do seem a little tense after such a long day."

Lyndon almost relented, then collected her thoughts. "I'll be all right, but I appreciate it." She tried not to notice the herbal fragrance of

Pella's hair hanging close to her—when had it come loose from its ponytail?—and her curves swelling and pressing against the rough garment.

"All right," Pella said, starting to back away. But her eyes searched Lyndon's face, and she stayed close. She knelt down in front of her. "At least let me take your shoes off, Miss, so you can relax for the night," she said.

Before Lyndon could protest, she took the heel of one shoe, leaning forward so her breasts brushed against Lyndon's knee. She took her time getting the shoe off and then moved over to the other leg, repeating the process.

Lyndon was helpless against the spreading warmth and excitement in her still new body. Between her legs a throbbing and gathering heat was both welcome and worrisome. She sat up straighter. "Um, thank you, very much," she said, noting her own voice sounded slightly huskier.

Pella took the shoes and set them by the door, bending over from the waist to put them down. Lyndon was riveted and flummoxed by this sudden change in Pella's behavior. Then the girl came back to the chair. She moved to pick up the mug of tea, at the same time insinuating one leg between Lyndon's so that she was standing straddled over her left thigh, her knee-length garment brushing Lyndon's pants leg. She leaned down slightly as she proffered the cup. "Don't forget about your tea, Miss," she said softly.

Lyndon couldn't pretend it wasn't happening anymore. "Um, Pella," she said. "I feel like you're, I don't know, trying to get me to cross a line here, maybe?"

Pella set the cup back down and stood where she was, her body swaying ever so slightly. "Do you want to cross a line, Miss?"

Lyndon groped for words. "I can't. It would be unethical, as an officer in an active investigation, and besides, the Mother Superior said—" she stopped as something else occurred to her; in her state she'd momentarily forgotten she was a woman. "And I thought you—I was under the impression you'd prefer the company of—well, that guy we saw at the resort, for example."

Something flickered over Pella's face, but it soon disappeared. "Well, as for what the Mother Superior said, I mean, she's right, we can't really give consent, but—if we're not the ones being asked that doesn't really apply, right? She'd never have to know—I wouldn't tell her; believe me, I'd be in much bigger trouble than you if she found out. And since this isn't being disobedient, my tracker won't register it as an offense unless I do something you don't want me to do."

She hiked her skirt up a little so Lyndon could begin to see her thighs. "And I might prefer men overall, and even have feelings for that guy at the resort, but there's no way I can risk being with one for a very long time, not until I'm a nun. But I still have needs."

She touched Lyndon's hand and, when she didn't pull away, took it and guided it to her own waist. "I've seen you looking at me, in a way that made me feel like you wanted me. And you've been so kind, Miss. You've made me feel a bit like a regular person again, and it's such a nice break."

She felt Lyndon's hand begin to tighten on her waist almost involuntarily and smiled. "So you don't have to get consent from me, Miss, but if you would want to, I would love to—share something tonight with you. Just this once."

Lyndon's mind with all its moral calculations shut off decisively. All she could feel was heavy desire for the inviting body standing in front of her. She put her other hand on Pella's waist and pulled the girl down so she tumbled onto her lap, a confusion of curls and curves and intoxicating scents and sounds.

Lyndon slid the hem of the dress up, caressing Pella's thigh as she did so, then moving higher and feeling a simple cloth undergarment, less coarse than the dress but not a rich fabric.

Pella shifted to allow the dress to be hiked up to her waist, and when Lyndon kept tugging it higher, raised her arms above her head so it could be slid off altogether. Her breasts, at least twice the size of Lyndon's, were bare under the garment, as were her feet—she'd slid her sandals off at some point that Lyndon couldn't recall—so she wore only the plain, modest white panties and, of course, the tracker around her neck.

Lyndon feasted her eyes and hands, and then her mouth, on the ripe curves, gradually ridding her of her last scrap of clothing, and Pella gasped with something like relief, squirming under Lyndon's caresses as if inviting her to squeeze harder, probe deeper, which she did. Pella worked her own hands under Lyndon's shirt and loosened her bra, lightly brushing the small, already erect nipples.

Lyndon moaned, overcome with dueling sensations of caressing a woman's body all over while feeling her own woman's body receive another person's touch for the first time. "Can we go to the bed?" Pella breathed into her ear, and Lyndon murmured assent.

They hurried over to it in a few strides and fell onto the soft bedspread together. Pella helped Lyndon dispose of the rest of her clothes so she was bare except for the bracelet-like device on her wrist. Pella stroked Lyndon's long, lean body and pressed her shorter, fuller frame against her.

Everything they did together was strange to Lyndon, with her memory of lovemaking as a man, but at the same time completely natural to the body that she now inhabited.

Sometime later, they lay side by side, their panting dying down as their breathing gradually returned to normal.

"Thank you," Lyndon said. She reached out and Pella came closer. Lyndon kissed the girl's irresistible lips over and over, then drew her even tighter against her. Later she would feel confusion and some guilt, but at the moment all she felt was sated.

* * *

Lyndon awoke. It was still dark, though a creamy moonlight glowed against her curtained windows. She scrubbed her face with her hand and rolled onto her back. Her nakedness, and the scents still clinging to her bedclothes, reminded her of what had happened.

She sat bolt upright and looked around; Pella was gone. Adrenaline coursed through Lyndon's body as she relived the sequence of events, hardly believing any of it. Though she was no longer sleepy, she changed into pajamas and got into bed.

No sooner was she back under the impossibly soft covers than there was an equally soft tapping on her door.

Lyndon flung the blanket off and stood again. Maybe Pella had returned for some reason. Or perhaps it would be the Mother Superior instead, ready to talk about the exposé.

She went to the door, unlocked and opened it, and was momentarily stunned at who was on the other side. Baffled, she waved her into her quarters.

CHAPTER TWENTY

Crystal ducked inside, still looking miserable, though much more collected than the last time they'd met. She avoided looking directly at Lyndon, and when she did, she couldn't disguise the resentment she was feeling. She stood just inside the door, hands folded in front of her.

Lyndon sighed tiredly. "How can I help you, Crystal? Please speak."

Crystal's downturned mouth twisted with bitterness, but she spoke promptly. "Miss, I found something I thought you would want." She held out her right hand; in the palm was a small scrap of the rough material used for postulant clothing, wrapped around a tiny object.

Lyndon took it from her and unfolded the cloth. Inside was a minute piece of plastic, less than a centimeter square. She held it up to the light, turning it this way and that. "What is it?" she asked.

"I think it might be the chip that was missing out of Crenshaw Connelly's head," Crystal said simply.

Lyndon was startled. "What? How did you find it? What's on it?"

Crystal hung her head for a moment, then looked up. "I don't know. I found it in the Mother Superior's office, and it doesn't fit any of her devices."

"How long have you had this?"

"I just found it, a few minutes ago."

"And what were you doing in the office this time of night, if you don't mind my asking?"

Crystal shrunk further against the wall as if she wished it would dissolve and let her melt through it. "It's complicated," she said.

"Tell me everything," Lyndon said.

Crystal sighed. "I've—been having doubts about things lately," she said.

"About what?"

"Well … it started when we found Ms. Connelly," Crystal started slowly. "Do you know the foundational statement of our order?"

"It's, uh—" Lyndon blanked.

"'Life is precious.' We try to do everything we can to preserve and prolong life. The environment, animals—it's why we don't eat meat—but especially human life. When a young healthy woman ends up dead on our grounds, even if she's a trespasser, that should be a huge deal. I didn't get the feeling the Mother Superior cared at all about her life. She was all concerned about our privacy, about the spa suffering from bad publicity, about letting an outsider in to investigate." Her eyes cut to Lyndon's and away again.

"When you—when my tracker went up earlier today, I thought about giving up. I really did. It felt like two years of insanely hard work down the drain, but if I quit, I could at least get paid for those years, and I'd be going back to Mars with some medical training. I'd still have a better life than before I came here.

"But then I heard about that interview." Crystal closed her eyes briefly. "We're pretty sure we know who 'Cat' really is—not that many postulants leave the order—and if it is who we think it is, she's not the most trustworthy person. But President Gorn is, and he must've vetted her story." Lyndon had her doubts about that but stayed silent, nodding to encourage Crystal to continue.

"And, even if she's exaggerating, we all kind of think there's at least some truth to what she said. And where does that leave me?" Her mouth twisted again, lower lip trembling. "Basically practicing medicine for years—in addition to being at every nun's beck and call—for free, with no hope of compensation unless I keep going for at least another nine years. I think that's called being enslaved."

Lyndon felt sick about her role in it, however necessary it had been to get information. But there was nothing she could do at this point. "So why'd you search the Mother Superior's office?"

"I thought I might find evidence of what payments have been made to postulants who left, see if it was as bad as Cat claimed. I didn't find any records of it, but I did come across that chip."

"How'd you know there was one missing from Ms. Connelly's camera?"

"Word gets around."

Lyndon nodded, turning the chip over carefully in her hand, eager to try and get into it. "Crystal, thank you for coming to me. I know it must have been hard, after—earlier."

Crystal looked into her eyes again, this time holding her gaze steady. Indignation burned in her expression. "I didn't do it for you. Miss. I did it for Crenshaw."

"I understand. I'm going to do everything I can to find out who killed her. And—" Lyndon hesitated over what felt like it would be an empty gesture, then continued. "I'm sorry about what happened earlier. If there is anything I can do—any way to undo it—"

Crystal shook her head. She started to speak but her voice cracked. She cleared her throat and swallowed audibly. "May I go now, Miss?"

"Of course. Thanks again. And if you find anything else out—"

"I know. I will."

Lyndon locked the door after Crystal and pulled her mobile out immediately, slotting the chip into a universal adapter, hoping it wasn't encrypted beyond her mobile's abilities.

After a few seconds of quiet whirrs and clicks, the chip was in place and the screen automatically opened in the air in front of Lyndon's eyes.

It showed a now-familiar view of the convent grounds near the entrance. A whisper that almost didn't sound like Crenshaw Connelly's voice arose: "I'm standing on the grounds of the Order of Halcyon as possibly the first outsider ever to step foot on them. I'm here to see what secrets I can uncover about this mysterious order."

The camera vantage point began to move, slowly, with frequent pans of the area as Crenshaw looked around, her breathing the loudest sound in the recording.

"The Halcyon resort does wonders for your body and mind; a week spent there takes years off your appearance and how you feel, no plastic surgery or gene therapy required. But for a long time I've heard rumors that the nuns—or maybe their planet—control even greater powers of healing and rejuvenation. That the Mother Superior is actually the same one who brought the convent here over a hundred years ago, yet looks like she's in her thirties.

"Imagine what that kind of power would do for the galaxy—virtually wipe out sickness and the ravages of age."

Lyndon was again struck by how different Crenshaw sounded. Her normally peppy, ditzy stream of patter had been replaced by serious, carefully articulated thoughts.

The whispered voice-over continued as the camera took a familiar journey through the grounds. "On the flip side, I've also heard claims of human rights abuses within the convent's walls. Everything from physical abuse to mental torture. So I'm also here to see if there's any evidence of that."

She was silent for a few beats as she looked around. "It's beautiful and peaceful here at night. From what I've seen of the nuns at the resort, some are clearly treated differently; they have inferior clothes and get ordered around by the others. But looking around, I see what looks like dorms, and they're all equally beautiful on the outside. Let's see what else we can find."

She moved along, the camera movement indicating furtiveness. Suddenly the view swung around, accompanied by a stifled shriek. Foliage rustled and Crenshaw laughed quietly. "Just an animal of some kind," she said, and kept moving.

Crenshaw walked over the part of the lawn that Lyndon recognized as where she'd met her demise. She passed the rock Lyndon knew led to the cave where the girl's body would temporarily be housed. It was evident from how the camera didn't linger that she couldn't see anything unusual or potentially significant about the boulder's face.

Now she was creeping slowly down the slight incline toward the larger pond where Crystal and her companions had held their ceremony. The camera zoomed in on the water, and Lyndon could see it more clearly than she had in person.

There was a quality to the water, even without the nuns' ritualistic motions, that was unlike anything she'd ever seen. Small white incandescent specks swam about in it, and the water itself moved in a way that seemed intentional, almost sentient.

"There's something very unusual about this spot," Crenshaw whispered, as if echoing Lyndon's thoughts. "The water is—"

Her words cut off abruptly and the camera view zoomed back in and swung around as she evidently turned back the way she'd come. As soon as she had, there was an audible thump and the picture swung wildly, going sideways and down.

CHAPTER TWENTY-ONE

Lyndon watched with a hollowness in the pit of her stomach, helpless in the face of the brutal attack. She occasionally saw patches of cloth and once or twice a split second of the attacker's hooded head and masked face. The mask completely obscured his or her face, including the eyes.

When the struggle was at last over, the recording ran through what had been transmitted to Earth. Lyndon now recognized Crystal when her face appeared after turning Crenshaw's body over.

Lyndon sent a copy of the video to headquarters with a terse message explaining its context. Then she returned to bed and lay under the covers, staring at the ceiling. She'd need to catch up on sleep at some point, but it wouldn't be tonight.

* * *

A message notification chimed on the mobile and Lyndon jerked awake. She tapped her device and the holoscreen appeared above it, filled with Stoughton's face. "Got the video. Great work, Bates. You'll have to fill me in later in more detail about how you got it. I'm sending it to the lab to enhance the video and see if they can pick out any part of the assailant's face."

Stoughton rubbed his bleary eyes; it didn't appear he was getting much more rest than Lyndon. "I'm sure you saw or heard about that stunt with Gorn and the anonymous what's-it-called, nun trainee or whatever. Well, check out the attached. Trailer for a new episode of 'Dear Leader' airing this evening. Live show. You'll want to see it. We're trying to find out more about it, but right now we don't know anything beyond the promo."

The Commander signed off and the video message ended. Lyndon played the attachment.

A black screen with odd shifting color shapes appeared, along with atmospheric music. A baritone male voice intoned, "Coming tonight, an episode of 'Dear Leader' like nothing you've ever seen before." Flashes of Gorn's face, eyes closed, against some sort of white backdrop, were intercut with equally fleeting glimpses of the Halcyon resort. "A live broadcast show that will change everything."

The screen went back to the shifting shapes. "President Gorn takes a stand." The screen cut to (and this time stayed on) a close-up shot of Gorn's face, eyes closed. Suddenly he opened them, staring straight at the camera.

"Tune in for truth," he said with an air of gravity. The promo ended abruptly and Lyndon's screen automatically disappeared.

Lyndon had just finished showering when she heard a light tapping on her door. "Who is it?" she called, hurrying to put on undergarments.

"Pella, Miss," came the muffled response.

"Just a minute!" Lyndon threw on pants and a shirt and came barefoot and wet-haired to the door.

Pella stood with a covered tray dressed in her customary uniform. Lyndon flashed to a vivid memory of tugging the garment over Pella's head and felt heat spread through her body as she averted her eyes from Pella yet pictured her body in stark clarity.

Lyndon held open the door. Pella smiled nervously and came in, looking guarded. Lyndon considered the precarious position the girl had put herself in. An unscrupulous person could wield their knowledge of the night before—and of Pella's inability to disobey direct orders—to take things farther than she wanted.

"I hope I didn't wake you, Miss," she said, and Lyndon could tell Pella was equally aware of the risk she'd opened herself up to. Lyndon resolved to make it clear, by acting as if last night had never happened, that she wasn't thinking about taking advantage of the situation.

"No, you didn't wake me," Lyndon said, trying to smooth out her damp rumpled hair. "I was just getting ready."

"I took the liberty of bringing breakfast like yesterday, Miss, but if you want to go over to the dining hall instead …"

"No no, this is great," Lyndon said. "Very thoughtful, Pella, thanks. I hope you brought enough for you too."

Pella smiled sheepishly. "Yes, Miss, just in case you wanted me to join you."

The postulant bustled around the small apartment while tea brewed, gathering discarded clothes and putting them in a hamper in one of the closets, taking the untouched mug of cold tea from the night before into the kitchen to wash it, straightening the bed cover and pillows.

Lyndon studiously occupied herself with toweling her hair dry and putting on socks and boots as the girl tidied away the evidence of their lovemaking.

By the time Lyndon had finished her brief toilette, her breakfast was waiting on the table by her armchair: a steaming bowl of what appeared to be a grain porridge topped with berries, and a thick slice of bread, toasted, slathered with more of the rich spread she'd had yesterday. Her mouth watered as she sat down and dug in. Pella brought her a mug of tea, then came in with her own breakfast and sat on the floor next to the chair.

"Have you heard about 'Dear Leader'?" Pella asked with nervous excitement.

"Yeah, word's getting around the convent too, huh?"

"One of the nuns was on cleaning duty at the spa and saw the promo; she came back and told the Mother Superior while Margarita—she's another postulant—was bringing her breakfast. Everybody's talking about it now." She paused, then added in a fearful voice, "What do you think it's going to be?"

Lyndon shook her head, mouth full of porridge and toast. "No idea," she said finally, after swallowing. "Guess we'll just have to wait and see."

She ran down the list of open leads while she finished breakfast: the body and crime scene scans and videos with headquarters for analysis. Hearing back about Connor Connelly's attempt to buy Halcyon. Trying to find out why the Mother Superior had stolen Crenshaw's chip; should she ask her directly or do some snooping first?

Lyndon felt her brain function was beginning to suffer from the two nights of virtually no sleep, so she decided to start with a nap. She sent Pella away after breakfast and lay back down. Sleep was mercifully quick to come, and deep when it did.

* * *

She woke only when Pella brought her lunch. She had several notifications waiting on her mobile by then, too, so she once again dismissed Pella and checked messages while she picked at her food.

The lab had analyzed the scan of the cave and tunnel; predictably there was DNA from dozens of people. Crenshaw's blood-soaked clothing came back with only her DNA, so no clues about her killer. Analysis of the stab wounds revealed she'd been killed by a standard laser knife, a common household tool.

However, there was much better news from the video analysis. The technicians had obtained a predictive illustration of the assailant based on the contours of the masked face. Lyndon sat up, suddenly fully awake.

The Commander had sent the photorealistic sketch, showing a young man with large, deep-set eyes and a slightly upturned nose. He'd also attached photos and video clips of one Lockwood Manette. The resemblance was striking, and so was his bio.

He was a drug addict with a criminal record. He was also an ex-boyfriend of Crenshaw Connelly.

CHAPTER TWENTY-TWO

Lyndon felt guilty for napping while all these messages were arriving. She contacted Commander Stoughton immediately.

She expected a scolding for being unavailable for hours, but Stoughton was too excited by the developments to even ask where she'd been. Manette had been easily apprehended at his Hollywood apartment, where he'd been sound asleep with his current girlfriend, and was being questioned. A search of his home had turned up a laser knife of the type that had been used in the murder, along with a stash of fink.

"His girlfriend alibied him, but she's not a very credible witness. They've both got rap sheets; minor offenses, mostly drug-related, but still."

"Crenshaw has a rap sheet too, sir," Lyndon said.

"Yeah yeah, I know it doesn't prove anything, smartass. The most compelling evidence, honestly, is that sketch. He's got a distinctive face and that thing matches him to a tee. And the fact he dated Crenshaw—it's too much of a coincidence to ignore. It was a huge upgrade for him, that relationship; he'd been a bit part actor and sometimes a model, but the publicity of dating Crenshaw landed him some decent gigs.

"His life pretty much went to shit after they broke up; he ended up worse than he'd been before he met her. Got into debt, started abusing drugs, couldn't get show biz work because of his erratic behavior, and eventually his looks started to go from the drugs and hard living. Can't you see him blaming Crenshaw for all that?"

Lyndon agreed it seemed like a good chance. "Only how'd he afford to get to Halcyon if he's in debt and spending everything on drugs?"

"We're gonna check for credit cards in his name, talk to known associates to see if anyone loaned him money. We'll figure it out. If he didn't do it, he didn't do it, but goddamn, he looks good for it!"

Stoughton had apparently forgotten or dismissed the significance of where the drive had been found, and with no solid theories of her own to explain it, Lyndon didn't bring it up. They ended the call, and Lyndon spent some time learning about Lockwood and Crenshaw's relationship from tabloids.

She studied pictures and video of the couple. Lockwood was about the same height as Crenshaw and usually looked shorter because of the tall heels she favored for red carpet events. During the relationship his pale face, large eyes and slight tilt to his nose gave him an elfin, almost angelic appearance, and he was usually looking adoringly at Crenshaw while she smiled or blew kisses at the camera. He was almost as slight as her too; he looked more waifish than wiry, though Lyndon supposed he could be stronger than he appeared.

In mugshots of Lockwood after their breakup—also readily available in the exact same tabloids that had fetishized the celebrity romance—he looked considerably less puckish, with dark circles under his eyes and gaunt cheeks, usually with a scrape or bruise visible on his face. It was certainly possible he'd been the assailant—Crenshaw's video as well as the evidence on her body had indicated she'd put up pretty good resistance—but even in his mugshots it was hard to picture him as a murderer.

Lyndon looked up prices of transport from Earth to Halcyon. Even when bundled with a stay at a resort hotel and spa treatment package, it was more than the average Earth citizen would make probably in three or four months.

As she was watching old videos about Lockwood's arrests on one of the tabloids, the promo for "Dear Leader" came on between clips, and Lyndon realized that the show would start in less than an hour. She kept an eye on time as she continued her research on Lockwood Manette.

At the appointed time, she turned the show on. If the murderer was Lockwood, someone not connected to the convent at all, then any revelations Gorn might have about the order would be superfluous to Lyndon's investigation. But it wasn't an open and shut case, and besides, at this point she knew enough about the convent to have a personal curiosity about what the show might reveal.

After the standard gaudy credits, the show cut to Gorn. His round face was solemn and he was shot in close-up, so whatever outlandish outfit he might be wearing couldn't be seen. Lyndon noted his baby-smooth skin and glossy black hair; no vanity wrinkles or silver streaks like Connor Connelly chose to have.

"My friends," he said, "the majority of tonight's show will be brought to you live, a simulcast that you will be able to watch as it's unfolding, in real time. But this portion is recorded, and soon you'll see why that was necessary.

"You saw in my previous episode how I began to unpeel the layers of dishonesty and deception that shroud the Order of Halcyon's true, rotten core. As you can imagine, they don't like it much that I'm doing this. I wanted to come to Halcyon so that I could follow in darling Crenshaw's footsteps, except in broad daylight, demanding access, demanding transparency of these monsters who took her away. But I knew that after last night's painfully honest episode, I'd never be granted admission to the planet, let alone the spa or the convent."

The camera began to pan out, and Lyndon gasped. She instantly recognized the unusual mesh tunic that Gorn wore. He was in a sterile white room, and he stepped onto a platform.

An attendant in white adjusted the device around him as he spoke.

"That's why I decided a drastic measure was called for. I knew they would never let me in, but I had the perfect disguise. I also knew if I pre-recorded the entire episode, the nuns of Halcyon would try to find a way to block its release, tying it up in court as long as possible.

"My friends, I didn't want you to wait months or even years for this episode that you, and anyone who loves the Connellys, deserve to be able to see. Now, they may try to shut down the simulcast, but at least you'll be able to see it happen. It won't happen shrouded in the secrecy of court motions and appeals."

He was by now fully hooked up to the selfer. "This segment is being pre-recorded because selfing takes time. I've asked my camerawoman to not cut away as she brings you to the other room where my new self awaits. What you see as a lifeless mannequin will shortly be me, coming to you live from Halcyon!"

CHAPTER TWENTY-THREE

The camera turned and went through a door to a similarly sterile room. On a table, fastened with restraints, lay a lifeless body dressed in a similar mesh outfit.

It was the figure of a taller, more slender and muscular younger man, with long reddish-brown hair tied back in a ponytail and a mustache and beard. The skin was pale, nose and cheekbones prominent.

A female voice spoke up, off camera. "We're about to end the taped portion of this episode. When we return, the remainder of the show will be simulcast. And President Gorn will have taken the form of this self."

The video cut off abruptly, there was a split second of blackness, and then the screen burst into colorful life. The previously lifeless figure was now a handsome, lively human being wearing a broad smile, dressed in skin-tight burgundy trousers and a white shirt unbuttoned practically to the waist.

"And welcome back, my friends!" he said, the voice different but the vocal mannerisms the same. "This is President Gorn, 'dear leader' of the planet Mars. As you watch this, I am live, standing on the streets of the Halcyon Resort on the planet Halcyon." He gestured and the camera zoomed out and surveyed the scene, the idyllic tree-lined walks and picturesque buildings that Lyndon knew well by now.

Lyndon stared open-mouthed at the image on the screen as the young redheaded man continued talking, a curious gaggle of resort guests gathering behind him, whispering to one another. She shook herself out of her temporary paralysis. For the first time, she pressed the summoning button on the wristband that had become a natural part of her over the past couple days and waited for Pella while the broadcast continued.

"What a beautiful place, right, my friends? I've been here many times and experienced the healing quality of this wonderful planet." The Gorn-self's smile disappeared with theatrical suddenness. "It seems impossible that it should be hiding dark secrets below its surface, but remember, that darkness is the product of humans. The gorgeous nature of Halcyon has no choice in the matter of who controls it and to what ends they use it."

The light tapping on the door was less hesitant than usual. Still holding her mobile, Lyndon ran for the door and threw it open. "We have to get to the resort, now," she barked. "Run and tell the Mother Superior where we're going, then meet me at the gate. Go!"

Despite her evident surprise, Pella reacted with admirable swiftness and raced off without a word in the direction of the Mother Superior's offices. Lyndon ran in the other direction, toward the gates, barely noticing the nuns and postulants who paused to gawk at her and the holoscreen following her in midair.

She reached the gate and paced for what seemed like forever, but in less than five minutes Pella was speeding toward her. "We're cleared to leave, Miss," she said breathlessly. She touched the wall and the invisible door slid open. They ran silently together, watching the show, toward the car-hailing station.

"People of Earth: I was once one of you, as were many of my fellow Martians, or their ancestors. And Crenshaw was a treasure to all of us. Are you going to allow this twisted religious cult to murder one of your best and brightest, beloved by all the galaxy, and carry on with their amoral system as if nothing had happened?"

More people had gathered around the Gorn-self, some looking surprised and amused, others scared or worried.

Lyndon and Pella reached the shelter and Pella slapped the call button. Another couple of minutes passed like an eternity until the car arrived and the two got in. The holoscreen came with them.

"It's criminal that this small group of nuns hoards this entire, incredible planet," Gorn continued. "Did you know that the resort and the main campus of the convent take up less than a hundredth of a percent of this planet? Fewer than a thousand women own an entire planet—a virtual garden of Eden—while billions of you on Earth and over a billion on my beloved planet Mars suffer and scrape by on inadequate natural resources.

"They've gotten away with it because people assume they're holier than everyone else, that they're preserving a sacred place for the greater good. What greater good—the right to pay exorbitant fees to get a small taste of Halcyon's healing powers at the resort, then get kicked out when your money is used up?

"My dear friend and producer, Connor Connelly—father to the beautiful murdered girl, as you all know, and I bet that's no coincidence—even offered to buy some of this amazing land a few years ago, to help make it available to more people yearning to breathe free. These selfish women turned him down. They want it all to themselves.

"They don't want anyone even stepping foot in their precious convent—a crime that, apparently, they think should be punishable by DEATH!" His voice rose to a bellow at the end of this tirade.

Pella looked at Lyndon with horror. "What's he doing?" she whispered. Lyndon put her finger to her mouth and Pella fell silent.

"People of Earth!" Gorn shouted again, wild-eyed. "Your government is acting like it's powerless against this small group of women. Your police force is complacent. This diseased order of nuns must be cut off at the root, so they don't feel emboldened by this murder to commit even more atrocities. It's up to you, dear friends! You must rise up! You must tell your officials that you require them to act. You have the power! Earth must demand justice! Halcyon must go!"

Pella gasped, tears welling in her eyes. Lyndon looked impatiently ahead; she could see the outlines of the resort buildings. It wouldn't be long now.

On the screen, a nun appeared: Officer Li. She put her hand on the Gorn-self's elbow and tried to speak to him calmly, but he tore his arm away from her. His eyes were zealot-bright. She gestured and two more women appeared, one on either side of him.

"You see?" Gorn screamed. "You see what they do to anyone who dares speak out against them?" The women put their hands on his upper arms and he struggled theatrically to try and free himself without success. "Tyrants!" he shouted, and the nuns hesitated as if taken aback. Suddenly he stopped struggling and stood up straight.

"Please," he said in drastically calmer tones. "It's all right, you don't need to hold onto me like that. I'm coming to the station and I'm going to plead my case there."

The nuns loosened their grip and he pulled away, straightening his low-open white shirt as he did. "Let's calm down," he said in a suddenly conciliatory tone. He finished tugging at his shirt and patted his trouser legs as if to straighten them too. He smoothed his pants pockets, slipping his right hand into one—then pulled it out and popped something into his mouth.

"There, you see?" he said. "Everything's going to be fine." He looked into the camera. "My dear friends," he said. "I have chosen to end the life of this self rather than be tucked away in a prison. I trust that the technology of selfing will work correctly and deposit me back into my body once this one ceases to live. Remember everything I've said, my friends. The order of Halcyon doesn't deserve Halcyon after what they've done. *You* deserve Halcyon. We all deserve Halcyon. It must be confiscated."

The Gorn-self began to shake and foam at the mouth. The nuns grabbed him by the arms again, seemingly to support versus restrain him this time. They caught him just in time as his knees buckled and he sagged between them, coughing and spitting.

CHAPTER TWENTY-FOUR

"Shit!" Lyndon cried. She saw her chance to interview the "dear leader" slipping through her fingers. "Goddammit!" She pounded the side of the car.

The car entered the main strip of the resort. Almost immediately it slowed because a large crowd had formed in the street. "Stop, stop!" shouted Lyndon. The car came to a screeching halt. Lyndon jumped out, pushing her way through the throng. When she reached the middle, the focal point of their downturned gazes, she saw the Gorn-self lying helpless, eyes already glassy.

"Help him!" she shouted. She knelt beside the body, clasping her hands and thumping on his chest in an attempt at CPR. "Gorn, stay with me!" She looked up at the officers standing frozen. "Do you have an ambulance? Can you get medical help? Hurry!"

Her words jolted them into action. One ran off while the other helped Lyndon perform first aid. Soon two paramedics appeared with a stretcher, carried the body to a vehicle, and drove to the medical center. The policewomen cleared the street and Lyndon and Pella followed the ambulance in their car to the center.

While they waited outside the room where doctors worked to save the Gorn-self, Lyndon pulled the show up on her mobile again. The cameraperson had melted into the crowd that had dispersed and was now focused on the exterior of the medical center.

Lyndon showed Li, who sent two nuns to try and apprehend the camera operator based on the angle of the shot. But as they appeared on screen coming out of the building, the camera moved away as the cameraperson dodged down an alley.

Lyndon's frustration boiled up; with no radio contact with the officers in pursuit, she couldn't tell them which way their target had headed. But shortly it didn't matter anyway, because the screen cut abruptly away from the point of view of the running camera person. What filled the shot now was President Gorn's real face, unconscious, eyes closed. The camera pulled back silently to show his entire body ensconced in the selfer.

The door to the room where the Gorn-self was being worked on opened. The nun in the doorway shook her head, pulling a surgical mask from her face. "He's gone," she said.

Then she spotted the screen that Lyndon, Li, and Pella were glued to. On it, Gorn's body spasmed, his mouth worked, and his eyes opened.

"My friends," he said, his speech slow and labored. "I made it back. I must go and rest now, so for the rest of our time today, we will replay this very important episode. Tell your friends and family to tune in. Together, Mars and Earth will win. Until next time." Gorn closed his eyes again, the screen went dark, and then a voice-over began to set up the rerun.

* * *

The rest of the evening was spent at the resort, going through the motions of crime scene procedure. Lyndon sent a scan of the lifeless self to headquarters for analysis, though it seemed quite clear what had happened. She interviewed witnesses who didn't share anything she didn't already know. By the time they'd learned his identity by checking security footage at the transport station, Gorn's cameraperson was gone, fled via transport back to Mars.

Her mind scrambled to connect the Mars president's stunt and incendiary rhetoric with their new suspect in Crenshaw's murder, with Connor Connelly's past attempt to purchase Halcyon—which Gorn had mentioned in his speech—and with the Mother Superior's theft and concealment of Crenshaw's video chip.

Had Manette acted alone or was he being influenced or bankrolled by one of those three? Would Connor sacrifice his daughter for the sake of forcing a real estate deal? Would Gorn?

As for Crenshaw, the footage from her internal camera seemed to suggest a sincere attempt at investigative reporting. Was that really her sole aim in breaking into the convent, or had she been looking for something else, something to help her father's interests perhaps? Was the Mother Superior capable of murder if she saw Crenshaw as a threat?

The lab analysis of Gorn's self soon came back from Earth. As had been obvious, he'd ingested a lethal, fast-acting poison. Since selfs were fully functional human bodies, the poison had efficiently shut down its organs and ended its usefulness, which meant Gorn's consciousness had reverted back to his own body.

As Lyndon reviewed the report, she felt a soft tug on her arm. Pella, wide-eyed. Lyndon had instructed her to wait in the lobby of the police station and had forgotten all about her.

"Connor Connelly's on TV," Pella said. "He's about to make an announcement."

Lyndon quickly closed the report and opened her TV viewer on her mobile. The screen showed Connor looking somber, his face seeming older and his eyes even more haunted than when Lyndon had met him in person just a few days before. He was light-years away from the smirking playboy and his gaggle of beautiful creatures that Lyndon was used to seeing.

"A lot has happened," Connor began simply. "A lot of things have changed. I've changed. As a result, I've decided to make some major programming changes, effective immediately."

He looked directly into the camera. "The show 'Dear Leader' has been canceled. There won't be another episode of it on my network. I'll be releasing a detailed statement, but in a nutshell, I won't support a show that promotes war between planets. And I won't tolerate a show that uses my name to do so, or exploits the memory of my daughter Crenshaw to do so."

He took a deep breath. "I've been guilty of doing that myself, but it ends now. I'm also canceling the new show, 'Who's Living la Vida Next?'. It was the worst part of me that greenlighted that show, and I regret it with every fiber of my being.

"Anyone who knows me knows I stay out of government and politics," he continued. "But President Gorn used my network to make some false claims, so I have to speak up. The police of Earth are not being complacent. Justice will be served for Crenshaw. But it won't come from fearmongering and spewing rumors. I ask you to respect my family and trust the police, and give us time to come to the truth."

He looked off camera and nodded slightly, and the transmission ended.

CHAPTER TWENTY-FIVE

When they finally got back to the convent, dinner was long over. Pella brought leftovers to Lyndon's quarters, then hurried off when she was dismissed, no doubt to spread the word about the tumultuous events of the day.

Left alone at last, Lyndon went through her messages, and read and watched stories about the huge upheaval of two of the biggest shows in the galaxy.

Her mind kept running through the web of interconnected people and their cloudy motives and intentions, getting no closer to clarity. Exasperated, she turned on Crenshaw's video and watched her creep through the moon-drenched grounds, listening to every word for a hidden clue that would unlock the truth.

As the camera view approached the large pond again, zooming in on the water's ripples and their curious shimmer and movement, Lyndon wondered again about the ritual she'd witnessed there. What was it about this body of water that made it behave the way it did? Crenshaw was clearly struck by it; was it linked to whatever she was searching for on the convent grounds?

Standing with sudden decision, Lyndon threw on boots and a jacket, concealing her mobile in an inner pocket, and slipped out of her apartment. The moon was half obscured, but she was now familiar with this area of the convent and needed little illumination to find her way.

Marveling at how quickly she'd become immersed in a new body, a new sex, a new planet, a new society, Lyndon began to feel as if she were moving through a dream. So when she thought she saw figures in the distance, beyond the pool of water, it seemed at first like a figment of her imagination. She came back to reality and realized there was more than one person out besides her.

She threw the dark hood of her jacket over her head to prevent her blond hair shining in the patchy moonlight and headed in the direction of the movement.

By the time she'd circumvented the pond and reached the wooded area where she'd seen the figures, they were out of sight. She moved between the trees, putting her feet down tentatively on the uneven, leaf-thick ground.

The overhanging branches and vines blocked out almost all light, so she moved by feel, trying to tell herself that the woods couldn't be very large, so that even if she felt lost, she'd be able to find her way out when she needed to.

Lyndon noticed a faint, moving glow in the distance. She followed it, outpacing it until she got close enough to see the source of the light: a lantern swinging from an upraised hand.

Now that she'd caught up with the group, she kept quiet and stayed at a steady distance from them as they approached a low but steep hill. She couldn't tell what they did to make it happen, but a section of the grassy rise swung inward, revealing a dark opening. The women ducked to enter, one by one.

The opening disappeared. Lyndon hurried across the open field and ran her hand along the spot where it had been. Soft damp grass was all she felt; no buttons, no seams where the door might be. She scaled the knoll and lay on her stomach on top of it, waiting and listening in the quiet night.

There was a faint vibration of the earth beneath her. The door opening again, Lyndon guessed. She pressed herself down as low as she could get, seeing the dim glow of the lantern and hearing low whispers.

The group of women walked away toward the trees, and Lyndon could see it was three nuns and three postulants—the same numbers that had been at the ritual.

When they were a safe distance away, Lyndon slid down from her perch and tried the entrance again. Confident she was now alone, she spent more time probing with her fingertips where she thought the edge of the opening should roughly be.

She detected an irregularity in the surface and ran her fingertips along it, tracing the shape. It was a door, but she wasn't sure how to make it move.

As she paced in front of it, trying to trigger something, she felt it begin to move inward, shuddering under her touch. Encouraged, she pushed hard on the firm, grassy surface, and it continued its slow opening.

She leaned her shoulder against it to try and move it faster, digging her boots into the ground for purchase.

The grassy door gave an unexpected lurch and she pitched forward into darkness. As she fell, she collided with someone else and landed on the ground on top of them.

"What the fuck?" A woman's voice, surprised, indignant, with an undercurrent of fear.

"I'm sorry," Lyndon said as she hurried to get off the slender body she'd unintentionally pinned to the ground. She pulled out her mobile and turned on a light that cast a glow throughout a small earthen chamber, looking down at the person she'd knocked over and holding out her hand at the same time to help her up. Lyndon saw her face and froze with shock.

After a brief hesitation, a delicate hand took hers and used it as leverage to get to her feet. Lyndon nearly pitched forward again, then recovered and pulled the woman up. She was dressed in velvety pajamas made of the nuns' preferred material, but she was no nun.

Even with her face free of makeup and her hair softer and frizzier without product, Lyndon recognized her right away. She said the name with bewilderment, her own voice coming to her ears as if from a great distance.

"Crenshaw Connelly?"

CHAPTER TWENTY-SIX

Lyndon didn't know how it could be, but it was.

Anyone else might have looked surprised at being recognized by a complete stranger. Instead, that famous face registered fear and suspicion, backing slowly away. "Who are you?" she asked.

Lyndon tried to gain her composure, though all she could think about was the corpse she'd examined mere days before, in another cave on convent grounds. "Uh, Bates. Lyndon Bates, ma'am, officer with the National

Police Force. From Earth, ma'am. Is that really you?"

Crenshaw relaxed slightly but still kept her distance. "Yeah, it's me. How do I know *you're* really a cop, though?"

Lyndon was glad she had her mobile and that her ID badge on it had been updated with her self's photo before she came to Halcyon. She showed it to Crenshaw with slightly shaking hands.

Crenshaw studied it and seemed convinced. "Okay. So what now?"

Lyndon's head was flooded with questions, but the first thing she needed to do was contact headquarters. She tapped her device, then swore as she remembered she could only connect in her quarters and in the Mother Superior's office. Out here her mobile was essentially a flashlight and camera.

"We'll have to get back to my room, ma'am," she told Crenshaw. "Come with me, please."

Crenshaw shrank back. "Why? Why should I go with you?" she said. "There's someone after me," she said. "They tried to kill me. They—" she stopped.

They did kill you, Lyndon thought, disbelievingly. Crenshaw caught her look of dismay and misinterpreted it.

"What, you don't believe me?"

It was impossible to fully process or comprehend what was going on. Lyndon's cop instincts came to the rescue, and her mind started working on the immediate situation at hand, pushing aside all her questions for the time being. "I do believe you, and I can help. But I can only reach Earth in my room, so we have to get there. Then I can get you out of here safely."

"What, out of Halcyon? Back to Earth?" Crenshaw backed farther away. "I'm not going anywhere, not until I find out what's going on here."

Lyndon's exasperation crowded out her bewilderment. "Are you—are you crazy? After what's already happened, do you really think you're equipped to play detective here? Do you know how much trouble you've already created with your little adventure?"

"Little adventure?" Crenshaw's eyes flashed anger. "You condescending bitch. There must be a reason someone attacked me. I've got to find out what it is!" She suddenly made a break for the entrance.

Lyndon leaped in front of the entrance, blocking Crenshaw from escaping. She couldn't believe she was arguing with a woman she could've sworn was dead up until a few minutes ago. And who was massively famous. But she couldn't lose sight of the fact that there were potentially murderers and body-snatchers on this idyllic planet. She thought fast.

"Look, I'm trying to find out what's going on here too, ma'am. We can work together, but whoever wanted you dead could still be out there. The place I'm staying is less than a mile from here. You'll be safer there while we figure out what to do. I don't think the person who actually attacked you is still here, but we need to be careful just in case."

She tried to suppress the irritation in her voice. She just needed to get the girl to comply and not pitch a fit that might bring half the convent out of their dorms before she had a chance to assess the situation. "Please, ma'am. Once you see the evidence I've collected so far, I think you'll have a better idea what it is you're searching for yourself."

Crenshaw still looked doubtful, but at last she relented and followed Lyndon out of the cave. "I don't know how to close it, do you?" Lyndon whispered.

The other woman shook her head. "I snuck up and watched them open it so I could do it myself, but I'm not sure how it works on the outside."

"We'll have to leave it," Lyndon said. "They'd find out you were gone soon anyway, right?" The moon had come out from behind the clouds and the land was bathed in light. She cocked her head for Crenshaw to follow and hurried across the open field to the trees.

In the small wooded area, enough moonlight got through the trees to make it less dark and treacherous than when she'd come through before. She saw light coming through trees at the other end of it. Crenshaw kept silent and stayed close.

They came out into the clearing with the pond. The moon shining on the surface had created the extra illumination that led them so easily through the stand of trees.

Lyndon stole a glance at Crenshaw, whose face registered recognition of the spot. They'd soon be on the other side, where Lockwood Manette—if he was the murderer—had made his first strike. Crenshaw bit her lip, put her head down and kept going. Lyndon's lingering doubts that this really was Crenshaw, and that it really had been Crenshaw who was killed, started to drain away.

They made it back to Lyndon's quarters without encountering anyone else. Lyndon unlocked the door and let Crenshaw slip inside first. She took a final look around to see if she could spot anyone who may have seen or followed them, but the courtyard was peaceful, the surrounding windows all dark.

She came inside and locked the door. When she turned around, Crenshaw was standing in the middle of the room, hugging herself, looking physically drained. Lyndon was amazed she'd made it all the way to the room without passing out. She was barefoot, Lyndon realized, and her feet looked cold and damp, with grass and leaves clinging to them. "Do you want to wash up and put on some warmer clothes?" she asked.

Crenshaw nodded, too tired to argue at the moment, and Lyndon went to the closet to pull out a long sleeve shirt, leggings and socks. She saw the bag that contained Crenshaw's cut and bloody clothes and shut the closet hurriedly, handing over the clothes and pointing her to the bathroom.

When Crenshaw had shut herself in the bathroom and the water was running, Lyndon pulled out her mobile to get in touch with headquarters. She tried Stoughton but the call failed. Lyndon swore and tapped out a text message instead and sent it. A moment later, a notification popped up that the text hadn't gone through either.

Crenshaw emerged and Lyndon put her mobile away hurriedly. "How are you feeling, ma'am?" she asked. "Do you need to lie down?" She gestured to her bed. Crenshaw was so jaw-droppingly gorgeous in person, even in her current condition, that Lyndon found it hard to look at her directly. She noticed the woman had cuffed the sleeves of the shirt and that the leggings were bunched up at the ankles. She looked even more delicate in the too-big clothes.

Crenshaw shook her head and perched on the side of the bed. "I've been lying down for, I don't know, days? Weeks?" She rubbed her forehead. "I've lost all sense of time."

Lyndon hesitated. "Do you have any injuries on your body?"

Again Crenshaw indicated "no." "I did have some really bad pain in places, but it doesn't hurt at all anymore. My back felt like it had, like, some wounds of some kind, but—" she lifted her shirt a few inches to reveal a smooth, slender belly, and twisted halfway around so Lyndon could see her side and back were also unmarred. It was as if the scorched holes made by the laser knife had never been there at all.

CHAPTER TWENTY-SEVEN

Lyndon asked her to tell her everything she remembered since she'd entered the convent grounds.

Crenshaw closed her eyes. "Everything is mixed up," she said finally. "I was walking around, getting video of the place, and then someone slammed into me out of nowhere. I kind of remember trying to get them off me, and then this pain, the worst … I can't even describe it.

"I was lying on the ground, I started to pass out … it felt like my heart was slowing down and I couldn't move or even yell. Then everything went black for a second, and when I woke up I was kind of half walking, half being carried somewhere, but I couldn't see anything. And then I woke up in bed in that place I was trying to get out of when you knocked me down."

Her eyebrows creased. "I kept falling asleep. I couldn't stay awake. I don't know how many days went by because I just slept through them. Every once in a while I'd wake up and somebody would be standing over me, speaking in some language I couldn't understand. I felt like they were hypnotizing me, making me fall back asleep.

"This last time I woke up when they brought me food, and finally I felt completely awake. I pretended to be sleepy though. I didn't trust them not to do it again if they knew.

"When they left I followed them down this twisty tunnel that was all made of dirt, and I hid and watched how they touched the wall to make it open. I copied what they did—I had to try a few times before it worked, but then it started to open. And all of a sudden you were there on top of me!"

Lyndon felt her face grow warm as she remembered the sensation of their bodies pressed together. "Sorry about that, ma'am," she said. "I thought I was the one getting the door open, so I was pushing on it to open faster."

Crenshaw gave a faint smile, a shadow of her usually exuberant on-air self. "That's all I remember, so now you have to tell me what *you* know," she said. "How long have I been gone?"

"From Earth? A little over a week."

She looked incredulous. "Really? Including the time I spent at the resort?"

"Yes ma'am."

"I feel like so much time has passed, like I spent weeks in that bed!"

Lyndon swallowed. "I think it was more like a day." She pulled out her mobile again.

"What are you doing?" Crenshaw asked suspiciously.

"I need to get in touch with Earth, ma'am, so everyone knows you're all right."

"No!" Crenshaw said sharply, but Lyndon touched the screen anyway, trying and failing to connect with Stoughton or headquarters. Crenshaw lunged at her and tried to grab the phone, succeeding in knocking it out of Lyndon's hand and onto the floor.

"If my dad finds out where I am he'll just want to drag me back home to keep doing that shitty show forever!" she cried. "I need to come back with something real, a scoop that shows what I can really do so he'll take me seriously."

Glaring at Crenshaw, Lyndon pushed her aside to retrieve her phone, nearly knocking the unsteady girl off her feet. She picked up her device, then sighed and shrugged. "I can't get my phone working right now anyway. Must be an outage. Maybe the Mother Superior—" she paused, thinking about the camera drive having been hidden in the head nun's office.

Crenshaw looked anxious. "No, I don't think you should tell her about me," she said. "I overheard some of the nuns talking in

English once when I was awake. While one of them was doing the chanting or whatever, I heard others saying something about how the Mother Superior hadn't wanted to help me. I don't know why, but I think they thought they were protecting me by keeping me there, hiding me from her. The way it sounded, I don't trust her. Although, I'm not sure who to trust here—" She broke off, looking pointedly at Lyndon.

"You can trust me, ma'am," she said. "I was sent here to find out who—what happened to you." She made several rapid calculations in her head. "I won't tell anyone here that I found you until we find a way to get in contact with headquarters back on Earth."

Crenshaw regarded her speculatively. "If you want me to cooperate with you, you're going to have to give me something, too," she said. She stepped close to Lyndon and tilted her head up to look in her eyes. Despite her annoyance, Lyndon couldn't help being struck all over again by the fact that she was alone in a bedroom with a gorgeous mega-star.

Crenshaw seemed to read something into her expression and a knowing half smile formed on her face. She raised her hand to Lyndon's face and traced her cheek and jawline with her soft, slender fingers, moving closer, so close Lyndon thought she could feel the warmth of Crenshaw's breath on her lips. "You like me, don't you?" Crenshaw murmured.

"Um, I—" Lyndon found herself tongue-tied and unable to move.

"I need to know everything *you* know," Crenshaw whispered, and Lyndon felt a tingle go up her spine. She closed her eyes, hardly able to breathe, convinced for a second that Crenshaw was about to kiss her. Instead, the girl gave her a firm pat on the cheek, almost a slap, and stepped back with a triumphant look of scorn. "Sorry, I don't go that way, officer," she said. Lyndon felt humiliation wash over her at being so gullible.

"Anyway, here's the deal," Crenshaw said as if nothing had happened, though there was an amused gleam in her eyes. "If I feel like you're being straight with me, maybe we can do things your way. If I don't, I'm out; I'll fly solo and you can go back to Earth yourself and tell them you lost me. Pretty high-profile case, I bet, huh? It'd be a shame if it turned into a high-profile shit show instead and ruined your career."

Lyndon's mouth opened but no words came. She felt the urge to arrest Crenshaw for being uncooperative, but she hadn't broken any Earth laws; she was the victim of the crime. A crime she didn't even seem to fully grasp the extent of.

Maybe that's what it would take to get her to take this situation seriously. Lyndon almost wished she'd been able to take a scan of Crenshaw's corpse before it disappeared, so she could've shown her photographic evidence of her own death. She'd do the next best thing, she decided.

"Fine," Lyndon forced herself to say, clenching her jaw to try and keep her temper in check. "I'll tell you everything I know. Let's start here." She went to the closet and got the cloth bag she'd hurried to hide before. She pulled out Crenshaw's clothes and spread them on the floor.

The girl stared at them, eyes darting to the holes, to where Lyndon had cut the catsuit to get it off of her, to the copious amounts of blood detectable even against the dark fabric. She reached out and touched, very gingerly, the stiffened, blood-crusted surface of the clothing.

When she looked up at Lyndon again, her gloating defiance had disappeared. "What happened to me?"

CHAPTER TWENTY-EIGHT

Lyndon explained everything from the discovery of Crenshaw's body to Gorn's stunt to Crystal bringing the missing chip from the Mother Superior's office to the arrest of her ex-boyfriend. Crenshaw took it all in quietly and with admirable calm. When Lyndon had finished, she asked to see the video her camera had taken during her attack and after her apparent death.

Lyndon hesitated only briefly. The procedural playbook had been thrown out so long ago on this case. She pulled out her mobile, which still had the chip safely inserted, and the screen popped up.

"Skip ahead," Crenshaw said impatiently as the footage started. Lyndon fast-forwarded until she saw Crenshaw's sped-up point of view begin to approach the pond, then set it back to normal speed. She mostly watched Crenshaw's face as she watched the video, struggling to keep her emotions in check.

As the attack came to an end and Crenshaw's labored breathing ceased to be heard, she covered her mouth, eyes glued to the screen. They both watched in silence as the view remained unchanged for a minute or two, and then came the shifting of blades of grass as she was turned over.

Crenshaw uncovered her mouth and gasped as Crystal's face came into view. "I know her!" she exclaimed. "She was there, in that cave! That's one of them!"

* * *

With some small measure of guilt at waking her in the middle of the night, Lyndon used her wristband to summon Pella. She met her at the door of the apartment after asking Crenshaw to stay out of sight in the bathroom with the door closed. She wasn't sure if the girl knew about Crenshaw's being alive and hidden, but if not, Lyndon wasn't ready to have news of it spread throughout the postulants.

"Can you get Crystal and bring her here, now?" Lyndon asked the sleepy, disheveled girl.

"Of course, Miss," Pella said, and hurried off without question or hesitation. Lyndon couldn't help the passing thought of how much easier things would be right now if Crenshaw were so amenable to following her orders.

A few minutes later, both Pella and an even more tired-looking Crystal appeared at the door. Lyndon sent Pella away with an order to tell no one; she hoped Pella's collar would force her to obey so gossip didn't start spreading like wildfire, as it seemed to do in the convent.

Crystal entered the apartment at her insistence, looking distrustful. Lyndon had her sit in the armchair and stood over her, arms folded.

"I need you to tell me your whereabouts tonight," she ordered.

Crystal's eyes flicked to the side almost imperceptibly. "I cleaned the health center around nine o'clock, went to the dining hall to find some food because I hadn't eaten dinner, did some … chores, then went to my dorm. A while later, Pella woke me up and told me you had sent her to fetch me."

Lyndon glared at her. "That's your story, huh? Did you forget any little details? Leave anything out?" She raised her voice and called toward the bathroom, "Come on out."

Crystal's eyes widened as Crenshaw emerged, though even in her shock she managed to stay silent.

"Okay, stop this bullshit about not speaking without permission. I want you to talk to me like a normal human being. You knew the subject of my murder investigation wasn't actually dead," Lyndon snapped. "You knew this and you kept it from me. Why?"

Crystal looked terrified, but stammered, "I was under orders from Sister Tully and the others that I couldn't tell anyone. I can't directly disobey a nun." She couldn't stop staring at Crenshaw. "How did you—"

"Escape?" Crenshaw said. "I managed. The real question is, why the fuck were you keeping me locked up?"

"Please, Miss, it wasn't like that," Crystal protested. "We were trying to help you. We were going to find a way to get you out of here once you were fully healed. Think of an explanation that protected us all. I—I thought you were still a lot weaker than you are." She faltered under Crenshaw's withering glare.

"I think now that we know, it's not disobeying the nuns to explain exactly what happened," Lyndon said, struggling to sound patient. "Crystal, you need to stop being evasive and tell me everything. How is she still alive? I know what dead bodies look like. I touched her; there was no way she had any life left in her. What's going on?"

Crystal thought about it, then nodded, looking defeated. "She was dead, Miss. We—we resurrected her."

CHAPTER TWENTY-NINE

The words hung in the air between the three women for a long moment. But once Crystal got going, the words tumbled out faster and faster.

The healing powers of the planet Halcyon and its inhabitants were beyond what anyone on Earth could have imagined. In the hundred-plus years since they'd taken over the planet, the nuns had become more and more at one with the planet, discovering its unique qualities that spread health and healing through any living plant or creature that inhabited it. Then they discovered the pond, or "wellspring" as they called it.

They learned over time, through trial and error, that it was the epicenter of this force. The nuns had discovered how to harness its power to go beyond healing and actually reverse the death process.

Since then, no nun had died unless she willingly chose to end her life, which occasionally happened. Funerals on Halcyon were joyous occasions, the culmination of a life spent in youth and health and only ended after feeling fully satisfied and complete. Any nun who died unwillingly, as a result of injury or the rare disease that the planet didn't naturally prevent, was brought back in a ceremony like that witnessed by Lyndon.

The powers of the planet aligned with and strengthened the central tenet of their religion: "Life is precious." They realized, however, that using it to save everyone in the galaxy would be impossible and trying would be ill-advised, and that otherwise they'd have to be selective, which went against their beliefs.

So instead they maintained the secret, but in the rare instance that a non-member of their order died on the planet, they were brought back to life, without exception. Recipients of this second chance were unaware of their death and assumed they'd been brought back from the brink, not resurrected entirely.

However, the Mother Superior had given strict orders that the nuns not revive Crenshaw. She said that since the video had been sent to Earth, bringing her back might endanger their long-held secret and therefore the security of the convent's hold on the planet.

"There've been rumors that people have tried to force us to sell the planet, and that we're having financial troubles," Crystal said. "We all understood the risk. Most nuns agreed with the Mother Superior's decision, or at least went along with it. But at the same time, without our belief that life is precious, what were we? Sister Tully and a couple others came to a few of us postulants they thought would be struggling the most with the decision, because they needed at least six participants in the ceremony to make it work."

Crystal's mouth twisted bitterly. "In a lot of ways, the Order of Halcyon isn't what it seems. The Mother Superior acts like everything's simple, black and white, but she's allowed little things to slide over the years.

"Even this, one of the main rules of the convent—" she touched her tracker, and Lyndon was surprised to see it flash 7 instead of 9 "—isn't totally set in stone. There are ways for the nuns to take years off, as long as no one else knew they were there, if they like you. Sister Tully did this for me when she found out what happened, because she knew I got them trying to protect her secret."

The number blinked off after a few seconds. "Over time you get less naive about this place. A lot of people aren't really here for the religion; they just want security. And once they learn about the eternal life, they really want to stay. Only a few postulants know about it, those who can be trusted with the secret. Otherwise, it would spread too quickly and get out of control. We wouldn't be able to take in everyone who wanted to join, and we'd know most of them had selfish motives.

"But the one thing I still believed in completely, the one thing that held this religion and this convent together, was that we would never let someone suffer or die on our planet. No matter what the risk, even if it destroyed us. And the Mother Superior betrayed that."

She shook her head. "I still worship our goddess, but how do we go on if our absolute leader can go back on our most fundamental belief?" Her eyes turned to Crenshaw. "Our faith is a higher authority to me than even the Mother Superior, so I obeyed that, went against her orders, and helped resurrect you."

There was silence as both Lyndon and Crenshaw tried to absorb Crystal's words. At last Lyndon asked, "Do you believe that the Mother Superior had Crenshaw killed?"

Crystal shook her head hesitantly. "I'm not sure of anything anymore, but I'd be very surprised if it turns out she did it. She was really upset about the bad publicity she thought the murder would bring, that it might expose our secrets. And why kill you?" she said, turning back to Crenshaw. "Why not just have you escorted off the premises? Even if she couldn't confiscate the footage, I think she'd've decided it'd be better to have some video record of our grounds slip out than have the entire planet Earth come down on us."

"Still," Lyndon said, thinking out loud, "now that you're alive, you actually do possess a secret the Mother Superior doesn't want getting out." She tried her mobile again and put it back in her pocket. A flash of paranoia suddenly cut through her frustration. "It's really weird that this happens for the first time only after I brought you back to my room."

She looked around the room, especially along the sides of the ceiling. "It's like someone knew I'd found you and wanted to stop us contacting Earth. I can't be sure, but if that's the case, the Mother Superior may be aware you're here and getting ready to stop us. I think we should go now, tonight." She braced herself for Crenshaw's inevitable argument.

"Maybe you're right," Crenshaw said.

Lyndon tried to hide her shock. "Good, I'm glad we're in agreement now. Crystal, can you open the gate and let us out?"

"I can do that, but I can't stop the alarm from being triggered when you cut across the grass to the car station," Crystal said.

"Where's my signal-blocker?" Crenshaw asked. "Did that turn up with the rest of my things?"

Lyndon shook her head. "We think it must have been stolen by your attacker; we haven't been able to find it anywhere."

"Okay," said Crenshaw, unfazed, "we'll have to go fast then, hopefully get to the resort transport terminal before anyone stops us." Lyndon, still surprised at her sudden turnaround in attitude, agreed.

The three left Lyndon's quarters together, walking quickly. As far as Lyndon could tell they were alone. "I'm coming back, once I get Crenshaw safely home and get through to headquarters to let my Commander know what's going on here," Lyndon whispered to Crystal when they reached the wall.

Crystal bit her lip nervously. "What should I say if they find out I'm the one who let you out?"

"Open the gate," Lyndon commanded harshly. Crystal flinched but did as she was told, flicking her hand, in some sort of pattern too quickly to follow, over the seemingly smooth surface until a crack appeared and then the door slid open.

"Sorry about that, but now you'll be telling the truth when you tell them you didn't want to open the door but I ordered you to do it," Lyndon said in a normal tone. "You had no choice."

Crystal took a deep breath, a hint of resentment back in her eye, but she held her tongue. "Yes, Miss," was all she said.

"Now get ready to run," Lyndon told Crenshaw. "Once the alarm trips they'll be after us."

Crenshaw nodded, and they bolted through the opening without looking back. They reached the car station in less than a minute and pressed the call button. The night was eerily silent but they knew the alarm had been tripped in the security center and the Mother Superior's office.

They soon saw headlights cutting through the dark toward them. The car hummed quietly up and they scrambled in, Lyndon giving a verbal command to head to the resort.

Crenshaw looked behind them. Seeing no one, she relaxed with a slight smile. Lyndon saw her tapping lightly on her temple, and at first it looked like a nervous tic. A moment later Lyndon swore.

"So that's why you were suddenly so willing to listen to me about heading back to Earth," she said. "Your camera's reactivated, isn't that right? You were able to tape everything Crystal said. Now you've got your scoop."

CHAPTER THIRTY

Crenshaw shrugged but couldn't stop her smile getting a little wider. "Does it matter why I'm going along with you, as long as you get your way? Besides, what if one of them killed me? Do they deserve to have me keep their secret?"

Lyndon stared out the window. Even though Crystal must've known and accepted the risk of telling Crenshaw what had happened to her, Lyndon was sure she was hoping the convent's secret could be contained somehow. Trying to imagine the rich and powerful of Earth, Mars and other planets not setting their sights on Halcyon once they knew what it contained … but Crenshaw had a point: Did the convent really deserve to keep such a thing to itself?

Lost in her thoughts, she didn't at first notice another driverless car coming from the direction of the resort toward their car. Even if she had, she might not have thought much of it. Until it veered into their lane.

The car they were in performed a defensive maneuver, turning sharply to the right, as Lyndon and Crenshaw instinctively grabbed onto whatever they could to brace themselves, but the other car took that opportunity to ram into the side. Lyndon felt a heavy pain in her back, stomach, and legs, but it started growing less intense almost immediately, slipping away along with her consciousness.

* * *

"Officer Bates?" The male voice came to her as if from a great distance. Each time her name was repeated, the voice sounded closer and clearer.

She tried to speak but felt as if her vocal cords hadn't been used in weeks. She cleared her throat. "Yes?" she said, then opened her eyes in surprise at the sound of her voice.

His voice.

Lyndon stared befuddled into the face of the same technician who had orchestrated his transition into his self days before. "What happened?" He tried to move but was still strapped into the machine, and besides, his limbs felt half numb and too weak to put up much of a struggle.

"You're readjusting to your body, so give it a little while. Considering how quickly you took to your self, it should only be a few minutes before you feel mostly normal." The technician sounded calm, though his white uniform was slightly askew and his hair stuck up in a rumpled cowlick in back. "Commander Stoughton will be here soon, so save your strength for talking to him. I'm just here to make sure your transition is successful."

His hand was busy on part of the device that Lyndon couldn't even try to see with his head restrained. Quiet electronic sounds seemed to tell the technician whatever he needed to know, because his head nodded slightly as he surveyed the screen. Lyndon closed his eyes again, his mind racing back over his final moments before losing consciousness. He wondered how the force had known to come rescue his self, and why they'd transferred his consciousness out of it.

His dazed mind turned with a jolt to Crenshaw. She'd been in the seat farther away from the car that crashed into them; was she injured? Had they rescued her and brought her back to Earth as well? He hadn't caught a glimpse of anyone in the car that hit them and wondered if Crenshaw's killer had used it to try and finish the job. Lyndon strained instinctively against the machine that held him immobile.

"Bates!" Stoughton's voice cut through his troubled thoughts and his eyes flew open again. "What the hell happened? Are you okay?"

"I—I don't know, sir," Lyndon said, hating the tremor in his voice. "All I remember is passing out when the car hit me. Who found me? How long have I been out?"

Stoughton's face was blank, confused. "What do you—shit, didn't anyone tell you?"

"Tell me what, sir?"

"The selfer's monitor alarm went off about half an hour ago, signaling you'd returned to your body. That means your self is no longer functional." He saw Lyndon's confusion. "You died, son. That's all we know."

Lyndon felt that like a fist to his gut as his dazed mind finally caught up to what had happened. A moment later, another realization hit him like the second of a one-two punch.

"Sir, I have to go back," Lyndon said grimly, working hard to speak rapidly through lips that felt like they were just waking up. "Crenshaw Connelly is alive; at least, she was. She was in the car with me when I died. I need to get back to Halcyon. Now."

* * *

There was no time to consider transitioning him to a new self, even if one had been readily available. Stoughton got on his mobile as he escorted Lyndon to Connelly's teleportation station.

"I haven't been able to get through to anyone in the Halcyon police force," Stoughton told Lyndon as he was readied for transport. "I'll work on getting permission to send reinforcements, but I can't risk breaking protocol and escalating this situation even more. You're the only Earth law enforcement official authorized to be on active duty on Halcyon right now."

"I understand, sir," Lyndon said.

"Ready in five," the transit official said, tapping on a screen only visible from his perspective. Lyndon closed his eyes and forced himself to relax as a computer-generated voice counted down.

"Welcome to Halcyon," another computer voice said warmly a second after Lyndon heard "one." He opened his eyes and an attendant helped him step out of the machine.

"Do you have a reservation, sir?" she said with a puzzled look at a screen where she was clearly searching for records of his scheduled arrival. He barely acknowledged the woman as he raced from the room and onto the street, where he hailed a driverless car and ordered it to go to the station closest to the convent.

His device rang. It was Stoughton. "I'm on my way, sir," Lyndon said.

"All right, keep me posted," Stoughton said. "I'm just calling because I didn't get a chance to tell you: Manette's got a pretty strong alibi. We're doing some more investigation to see if it holds up. If it does, must have been his goddamn lookalike that attacked Crenshaw."

"Damn. All right, keep me posted, sir." Lyndon disconnected with a frown. He watched out the window as they drove. When the car came to where the accident had been, on one side of the road he saw torn-up grass, wheel marks in the rich dark soil, and some small fragments of machinery, but no sign of the vehicles or bodies.

The car reached the last station, where the road ended. There was no manual override of the car's automatic controls that could force it to keep going over the grass, so Lyndon had no choice but to jump out and race across the field toward the seamless wall of the convent. He banged on the solid-seeming surface, shouting to be let in.

Almost immediately the wall slid open a crack. "Who are you?" asked a voice on the other side. Lyndon thought he recognized it as belonging to a member of Halcyon law enforcement, but he could see nothing through the slim opening in the thick wall.

"Officer Lyndon Bates," he said.

Silence on the other side. Lyndon swallowed. "Look, I can explain. I was using a—"

"We know," the other voice said flatly.

"You have to let me in," he said, knowing he didn't have the authority to make them. "I apologize for my deception, but—the damage has already been done, right? I've already been inside." He thought of Crenshaw and panic rose in him. It wasn't just about his job, he realized. Helplessly, he tried again. "I need to find out what happened to Crenshaw."

He heard murmurs through the crack that he couldn't make out. The wall began to swing open and relief flooded his body. The nun on the other side, who was indeed one of the police officers who had been present at the Gorn debacle, looked him up and down, her lips tightening with disapproval at the firearm strapped to his chest. He expected more surprise at his altered appearance, but she simply stepped aside and gestured for him to pass through the gate.

"Do you know where Ms. Connelly is?" he asked the nun.

"I'll take you to Li. She'll fill you in," the woman replied curtly, and took off at a brisk pace. Lyndon hurried behind her without objection.

He was led to the Mother Superior's office and told to wait outside while the nun went in and closed the door. It reopened almost immediately and she ushered him in.

To his surprise, the Mother Superior wasn't there. Li sat at her desk, flanked by two of her officers. On a small sofa on the side of the room sat Pella, Crystal, and a nun Lyndon recognized from the resurrection ceremony. Crenshaw was nowhere to be seen.

Li looked him up and down with impassive eyes. "So you're Lyndon Bates," she said.

"Yes ma'am. I'm sorry for the deception, but—"

Li stopped him with a lifted hand. "We have enough to discuss without going into that," she said.

"Yes ma'am," Lyndon said, relieved. "Where's Ms. Connelly? Is she okay?"

"Not at present," Li said, her terse tone belying her words. "Ms. Connelly passed away as a result of her injuries from the crash, along with your self."

CHAPTER THIRTY-ONE

Lyndon reeled back, stunned.

"Both bodies are under guard, and I can take you to them shortly," Li continued. "We knew there was something off about your self's body when we checked it, and after President Gorn's recent stunt it wasn't hard to figure out, but we retrieved it anyway and put it into cold storage with Ms. Connelly's, as evidence."

She paused. "You might be wondering where the Mother Superior is." Lyndon assented wordlessly. "She's been detained under suspicion of murder. I've taken over leadership of Halcyon in the interim, by consensus of the senior members of our order, until the situation is contained."

"What—how—" Lyndon had so many questions he couldn't figure out how to put any into words.

"I'm nearly certain the Mother Superior caused the car crash," Li said. "The only way I can think of for that to have happened, an empty car crashing into another, was through her control center." She gestured at the desk. "She must've come in after I left the office that night and seen you with Ms. Connelly in your room."

Lyndon opened his mouth, but Li continued before he could ask a question. "The Mother Superior was monitoring your quarters by video surveillance." Even though he'd suspected it at the end, Lyndon felt his face grow warm to have his suspicion confirmed, especially when he considered what had gone on in his quarters. Pella's presence just out of his peripheral vision was suddenly palpable, and he wondered whether she'd already dealt with the embarrassing realization.

And he suddenly wondered what she thought of it in retrospect, now that she knew he was a man. But there was no time to dwell on it as Li continued.

"I happened to be in here, taking care of other business while she was out, when I saw you on the screen, entering your apartment with Ms. Connelly. I wasn't sure what had happened or what you planned to do, but I disabled connectivity in your apartment at once until I could straighten it out. I wanted to make sure I understood the situation before you got your superiors on Earth involved.

"I saw Crystal arrive, and I apprehended Pella after you sent her away to find out what she knew. She of course knew nothing about Ms. Connelly being in your room, and by the time I got to your quarters, you were gone.

"One of my officers alerted me that the alarm had been triggered. We called a car and headed toward the resort, where we assumed you'd be going, and came across the scene of the crash. You were both crushed inside your vehicle and there was no one in the other car.

The vehicle was totaled; we didn't think anyone could have survived the impact if they'd been inside it. We had the cars and bodies transported back here. They actually only got here a few minutes before you returned.

"Meanwhile, I convened an emergency meeting of the senior members of Halcyon. Several of them already had their doubts about the Mother Superior's leadership, so it didn't take long to decide she needed to be removed from power, at least temporarily, while we investigated."

Lyndon scrubbed a hand over his face, only half registering the strangeness of his rough chin after days of living with a feminine face. "Do you think the Mother Superior had anything to do with Ms. Connelly's murder? I mean, the first time around?"

Li held a similar view to what Crystal had expressed earlier, and Lyndon agreed that it wouldn't have made sense for her to take such extreme measures at that point, even if she were capable of such a cold-blooded act. "And besides, she's confessed to tonight's homicide," Li said. "Why would she bother to deny responsibility for the first time?" That meant the original assassin's identity was still a mystery, unless Manette's alibi could be disproven.

"I need to question the Mother Superior," Lyndon said firmly. "And please contact my commander to authorize more officers. I'm going to need backup to clean this mess up."

"Of course," Li said. "We're fully cooperating with your investigation."

Li and the other two officers led Lyndon from the office to a door at the end of the hall. Li unlocked the door and accompanied Lyndon inside while the others stood guard outside.

The room was dim, the curtains closed. The Mother Superior sat stiffly perched on the edge of an armchair. Her hands were bound with glowing force-field cuffs. Lyndon saw a similar glow on her ankles. She looked at him without interest, looked away. "Now we're letting men on the premises, I see," she said to Li. "It didn't take long for our standards to start suffering."

She held her wrists up, addressing Lyndon this time. "Over a hundred years I've devoted to creating a safe, comfortable and holy space for my order. This is how it ends."

Lyndon felt fairly confident she didn't recognize him or know who he was. "I'm from the National Police Force on Earth," he said. "I need you to tell me what happened here, starting with when Crenshaw Connelly was stabbed to death."

CHAPTER THIRTY-TWO

The Mother Superior looked morosely at the window, though the thick, dark curtain made it impossible to see anything other than a dim glow around the edges, indicating that dawn was beginning to break.

"I've always been able to fend off people interested in our planet. Ever since I discovered its powers—did you know I founded this convent?"

"There have been rumors," Lyndon said. "How did you discover it?"

She turned to face him, though her eyes were fixed on a distant spot somewhere behind

Lyndon. "I was a biophysicist for a company visiting unexplored, unused planets owned by Earth and assessing them for their natural resources and commercial potential. I was assigned to this planet back when it was called by a long string of numerals. It looked barren when we landed, and the rest of the crew, even the other scientists, dismissed it outright once they scanned it and tested the soil for valuable or unknown minerals.

"I was ready to give up on it too. I was driving back alone in a solo pod after having searched in vain for signs of life. The vehicle hit a large hole I didn't see in time and crashed. I was unharmed, but while examining the exterior for damage, I cut my hand. It wasn't severe and I was in a hurry to get back to the ship, so I ignored it. The pod was half-buried in the dry dirt, so I began digging the wheel out with my hands." She looked down at them as if remembering. The edge of the glowing cuffs were just visible beneath the long sleeves of her robe.

"Some dust landed on my scratch, but it didn't cause any discomfort. On the contrary, my hand stopped hurting, and as I watched, all evidence of the wound gradually vanished. I knew I'd found something different from anything humankind had ever encountered.

"By the time I'd driven back to the main ship, my mind was made up. I told the rest of the crew nothing about my discovery, and we crossed this planet off our list of prospects for the company. I thought about what I could do with it. I secretly visited it several more times. I almost bankrupted myself—interplanetary travel was even more costly back then.

"But Halcyon's powers were undeniably unique, and gradually I formed a vision of a utopian society; as the holder of the planet's secrets, I could become its leader. I knew about the order of Halcyon and its devotion to sustaining life above all, and one day it came to me: Why not take an already disciplined, hard-working, and tight-knit group instead of trying to build a society from the ground up?

"It only took bringing their main healer to the planet and demonstrating its power. She recognized its potential, and the others were soon convinced. They'd received a sum of money from a wealthy supporter who had recently passed away. We had just enough to purchase the planet.

"I knew we'd need labor that we couldn't afford to make the planet habitable. And we needed to guard our secrets closely, so we couldn't hire outsiders. Instead, I helped reshape the requirements for postulants. As I predicted, my knowledge of the planet's powers gave me considerable sway within the order.

"We moved here with only enough supplies to last a few months, but with our labor force and our strict new laws of obedience, it didn't take long to grow our first crops and start fashioning the natural stones into buildings. It was easy to tap into Halcyon's power to create what we wanted. And once we released the latent energy that had been trapped within the planet for goddess knows how long, we helped it become a verdant paradise.

"Its gifts were so abundant and life here so pleasant that soon the reigning Mother Superior was deposed and I was put in her place. I gained absolute power over the Sisters of Halcyon with no force or violence."

"Very touching," Lyndon broke in. "Yet somehow you decided it was just fine to stab Crenshaw Connelly to death?"

"I didn't stab Ms. Connelly," the Mother Superior said, her tone so clipped it sounded like she was biting off the end of each word. She suddenly stood, and Lyndon stepped back instinctively. She was a tall woman, and she somehow seemed even more imposing despite her bound wrists and ankles.

"But I knew our home's powers would be coveted by every government, every rich and powerful person, who knew about them. So I've guarded them as much as possible. The resort was our way of giving back, and an important source of income. But it allowed people a glimpse of what we and our planet were capable of. It made them curious. And covetous. I should've known I couldn't keep people from wanting Halcyon for their own.

"I'd always managed to keep would-be buyers at bay. This last person, however, was relentless."

"Who?" Lyndon asked.

She shrugged listlessly. "I never found out. But he wouldn't leave me alone. And I don't know if he was responsible, but our financial troubles started a few months after he started calling. The resort wasn't pulling in as much money, the materials we needed to import became more expensive, wages kept going up. We'd been drawing slowly on bequests left to us by supporters on Earth, and we started draining it faster.

"I really thought we could make it, if we reallocated our postulants. But we were on the edge. We couldn't afford any bad publicity. And then this murder happened, at the most inconvenient time possible."

She sighed. "I didn't want to forbid Ms. Connelly's resurrection. It gave me no pleasure. But it was an easy decision: one trespasser's life or the existence of the institution I'd built."

She looked briefly at Lyndon, no recognition in her eyes. "I assigned one of my most libidinous postulants to the officer you sent, hoping she'd cause a scandal I could use to end the investigation early. I was not disappointed in her performance nor in your officer's gullibility—they jumped into bed practically the first moment they had alone—but then the damned corpse disappeared and that plan went out the window.

"I knew some of my followers had gone against my orders. I didn't know where they'd taken her, though, so all I could do was wait for her to show up. I had a feeling your officer might be approached by the traitors, so I decided not to expose her indiscretion with the postulant."

Lyndon knew his face had turned scarlet. He couldn't look at Li, who stood stoically beside him.

"Sure enough, the resurrected found her way to the officer's apartment. I had to stop them. Crenshaw had already been killed once, and police officers take their lives into their own hands as part of the job. In the larger picture, it wasn't as big of a sin as abandoning our entire religion would've been."

She shook her head. "If only I'd known that Li had been in my office before I got there, that she knew about them too. I could've covered my tracks if she hadn't been out there so quickly."

Lyndon felt cold rage, not as much for his destroyed self as for Crenshaw. "How would you have done that?"

She smiled a little. "I had the footage of my postulant and your officer. Then I had the officer running off with an even more beautiful, not to mention rich and famous, young woman. I was going to frame the girl, Pella, as having killed her rival and the woman who jilted her. But then I learned she'd already been taken into custody for questioning by Li's officers, so I couldn't make it seem like she'd used my control center to send the car after them."

Lyndon was shaking with anger. "How many people's lives would be an acceptable number to destroy to save your convent?" he said. The Mother Superior didn't dignify that with a response. "As one of your victims, I'd really like to know," he gritted out between clenched teeth. He pulled out his mobile and flashed his ID, which still had his female self's face on it. "I'm Lyndon Bates."

Her face went through a number of microexpressions before settling back to studied indifference. "Well, then, even that really wasn't murder at all," she mused. "Nice to know."

"In the eyes of the law it was," Lyndon said. "We've got more than enough evidence to extradite you and lock you up on Earth for the rest of your life."

For the first time, fear showed through cracks in the Mother Superior's exterior. "That's as good as a death sentence, you know. I won't last a year away from Halcyon."

Lyndon shrugged. "You've had a good run," he said, callously and with relish.

Mother Superior turned to Li. "You won't stop this?" she said with an edge of desperation. "I suppose 'Life is precious' has gone down the toilet with the rest of what we stood for?"

Li stared coldly. "You're the last one who should be talking about that, Deena," she said.

The woman's eyes darted from side to side as if looking futilely for an escape. Then she drew herself up. "Have you given up finding the original killer, then? You know I might be able to help with that."

Lyndon rose to the bait. "No need. We're hot on his trail. It's only a matter of time."

CHAPTER THIRTY-THREE

The shades were drawn in the small apartment. The air was fragrant with herbs, sweet and bitter and pungent, blending into an unfamiliar aroma that to Lyndon seemed exotic, almost magical.

A young postulant on a stool at the foot of the bed looked up from a book.

"How is she?" Lyndon said in a hushed voice.

"She's coming to, sir," the girl replied. "She's been stirring a little."

Lyndon got closer. Crystal had said the recovery should be faster this time, since her body hadn't sat for days before the ceremony, but he wasn't sure what to expect.

Crenshaw's face looked peaceful, her skin radiant even in the dim light, despite some cuts and bruises that looked to be healing. Her lips moved as if she were saying something in her dream, and then her eyelashes fluttered and her eyes opened.

She registered no recognition as Lyndon bent down a little, feeling uncharacteristically shy and flustered. "Guess you've got nine lives," he said lamely.

Her eyebrows drew together and she shook her head as if to clear it, then sat up in the bed, her shoulders looking thin and vulnerable as the blanket fell away. "Who are you?" she said weakly.

Lyndon reintroduced himself, showing his identification, and briefly explained. Despite her condition, a glimmer of Crenshaw surfaced. "Wow, your self made you seem more …mature," she said teasingly. "You're just a baby! I can't believe they sent a kid to solve my murder."

Lyndon's face grew warm and he stammered, which made her laugh.

"Relax," she said. "I'm sure you're very good at what you do—although you *did* get us both killed, now that I think about it." She yawned, remarkably unfazed, while he searched for words. "Just don't let it happen again, okay?" She leaned forward, looking fully alert. "Speaking of that, have you found my killer—either of them?"

Lyndon found his voice again. "I can't discuss anything right now," he said firmly, attempting to sound authoritative. He stood, suddenly aware that his superiors on Earth were waiting to learn what had happened. "I should know something soon."

* * *

Stoughton was at first stunned by the revelation about the Mother Superior, but that was soon overtaken by elation when he learned Crenshaw was alive. "You're going to be famous once this story hits the news; you know that, right?" he said gleefully. "She's all anyone can talk about. You're gonna get a hero's welcome back on Earth." Lyndon imagined Stoughton's relief that he could give his new friend Connor Connelly the good news.

"We'll get the ball rolling on extradition to Earth," Stoughton said. "Connor'll help me get the red tape out of the way." Lyndon barely kept a straight face at Stoughton's excitement to be able to say his name so casually.

"Bad news for your other investigation though," the Commander said. "Manette's alibi checks out. The harder we tried to poke holes in it, the more proof we found that he was where he said he was. We're back to square one on the first murder—attempted murder—whatever."

Lyndon swore under his breath, but by the time Stoughton was done talking, he knew what he needed to do. "Let's hold off on that extradition, and keep the press away from this story—and this planet. That includes Connor Connelly," he said firmly. The Commander started to protest, but Lyndon cut him off and explained his plan.

CHAPTER THIRTY-FOUR

Deena watched the man enter her office—the one she kept at the resort for meeting with outsiders—with a guarded expression. He was tall, tanned, and lean, with dark hair that came to his collar and swept across his forehead, almost into his eyes. He wore a friendly smile, but his eyes glittered with something else.

"Thank you for meeting with me, Mother Superior," he said in an ingratiating tone as he reached for her hand and shook it firmly. "The name's Stark."

"To be honest, I had very little choice in the matter," Deena said coldly. "Your request comes at a difficult time for Halcyon, otherwise we might not have entertained it. Ah well, that's not your fault, so I won't bore you with the tiresome details. Have a seat."

He lowered himself gracefully into a chair facing her.

"I have to admit, I'm pretty curious about what's changed," Stark said. "I was surprised you contacted me. You've been so … reticent to take my calls in the past."

Deena sighed heavily, with an attitude of resigned defeat, and turned to look out the fourth-floor window. Outside, the trees and their drapings of vine were silhouetted against a bright orange sun quickly sinking toward the horizon. The lights of the resort began to twinkle on a few at a time, and the interior lights of the office gradually brightened to counteract the dimming of the natural light coming in.

"I'm sure you heard about the unfortunate incident that happened on convent grounds. As terrible as that was—the killer is still at large!—it seems to have created a snowball of ill fortune for the convent. I don't know if you follow the news, but we've faced slander from all sides, including former convent members and even a world leader."

"Goodness!" the man exclaimed. The word and the way he said it were an odd fit with his rugged appearance.

"Yes," Deena said with another sigh, returning to her seat. "The scandals couldn't have come at a worse time; we were already struggling to stay afloat, and now bookings at the resort are down considerably, and we've cut all the expenses we already could. I need to look at more drastic measures, or else face the complete dissolution of our order."

The man put on a show of sympathy. "While I'm happy you're considering my offer, I'm so very sorry it's under such difficult conditions. I hope we can come to an agreement that is satisfactory for both of us."

Deena nodded. "I appreciate it." She squared her shoulders in a resolute manner. "I suppose we should talk specifics."

"Certainly," Stark said with a cordial air. "Well, as I've mentioned in our previous exchanges, I'm prepared to make you an exceedingly generous offer for the sale of your planet to me." He took out a mobile, touched the screen and held it out to her so she could see a figure on it. Deena looked at the number, and she didn't need to feign her astonishment at the amount.

"As you can see, it would dwarf any of the bequests you're rumored to have received from some of your benefactors—who, I've heard, have dwindled in number over the time you've been here. It would be more than enough to re-establish your order on another planet, where you could purchase enough land to live happily at a fraction of the profit you'd make from selling this one to me.

"I am a great admirer of your environmental stewardship of Halcyon and assure you that I'd hold myself and my operations to equally high standards. This is indeed an Eden, and sullying it in any way could not be farther from my mind."

Deena took a deep breath. "That's—a more than fair offer, Mr. Stark. I truly hope we can come to a compromise between what you want and what we want."

He pocketed his mobile device and sat back with a smirk. "Absolutely, my dear. I realize this is a negotiation, and I'm very interested to hear your counter offer."

"As you know, over ninety-five percent of this planet is undeveloped." He nodded. "Were you to make a binding contract with the convent to only use it according to certain sustainable specifications, we would be willing to sell you the vast majority of the land. We'd only retain the small portion our convent and resort are located on. I understand this would mean a decrease in your offer amount, but hopefully we could find a number agreeable to both of us."

Stark's smirk had faded as she spoke. With an evident effort, he kept his pleasant tone, but there was a hardness behind it. "While I know it would be hard to move, I submit you could start a new resort and build new convent grounds on another planet with the money I've offered. I'd even consider upping the amount to cover moving and building costs. But my offer is for the entire planet."

Deena sat in silence for a moment. "I see," she said. She rose and stood by the window again, looking out over the main street of the resort. Finally she turned back to Stark. "The resort is a vital part of why you're interested in Halcyon. I understand that. Very well, we'd entertain an offer that included the resort as well. All we would ask is to keep the small number of acres our convent is on.

"Perhaps it seems like sentimental nonsense to you, but for us, that little plot of land has become deeply spiritual. It's a part of our religion now, and we couldn't imagine our lives without it. You wouldn't miss it, and we'd be very reclusive, so we wouldn't bother whatever venture you chose to use the planet for. And you'd have a readymade income stream in the resort. Really, it could be much more profitable for someone who could afford to make some upfront investments."

Stark had stood too, moving closer to Deena as she spoke. Now he stood less than a foot from her. They stared at one another, Deena with her features as cold and expressionless as marble, Stark's eyes flashing with irritation.

"You need this deal," he said between gritted teeth. "You need it more than I do. And you don't get this deal if it isn't the whole planet." He leaned in so their noses were nearly touching. "What'll it be?"

Deena held his glance without flinching or moving backward. "Well, unfortunately, it appears we're at an impasse," she said. "We'll continue to seek another solution to our financial crisis. I'm very sorry to have wasted your time, Mr. Stark."

He stood for a second, then gave a barking laugh and shook his head. "No," he said calmly.

CHAPTER THIRTY-FIVE

Deena looked confused. "Excuse me?"

"NO!" Stark screamed the word this time, flecks of spittle landing on her face. "You will NOT stand in my way!"

"Why does it matter so much, Mr. Stark?" Deena asked, seemingly unfazed by his outburst. "Demanding a tiny plot of land versus owning nearly all of a beautiful planet. How could this term bother you that much?"

"You know why!" he shouted. "I know what you're hiding there, what you selfish bitches are trying to keep to yourself. How old are you? Huh? A hundred? Two hundred? You know what I want! Give it to me!" Before Deena could react, he had his hands around her throat. His eyes widened until they were practically bulging from their sockets. Deena managed to knee him in the crotch and send him stumbling backward, but he flew toward her again with uncontrollable rage.

Lyndon burst from his place of concealment in a recessed alcove behind a heavy curtain. He slammed into Stark, and both of them fell to the floor. Stark threw Lyndon off and scrambled to his feet, backing away, his breathing so guttural it was almost a growl. Despite his lean, strong body, Stark's movements were clumsy, his blows wild and inefficient, his reaction time slow. He clearly didn't fight very often.

Lyndon put himself in front of Deena and poised for another attack. Stark took one step, then paused, staring fixedly at a point behind them. Deena couldn't resist a glance back, but there was nothing there. She turned back, expecting Stark's next onslaught, but he was still standing stock still. As she and Lyndon watched, puzzled, he collapsed glassy-eyed to the floor.

Lyndon approached Stark cautiously, bent down and felt for a pulse. "I think he's dead!"

He tried opening Stark's eyes and felt for perceptible breaths, just to be sure, but the man was lifeless.

A commotion was heard in the corridor outside the office, and the door burst open. A convent officer came in. "The news!" she blurted. "Right now!"

Lyndon pulled out his mobile. The holoscreen appeared and on it a serious-looking newscaster with the words "breaking news" flashing behind him. "I repeat, we've received word that President Gorn of Mars, former star of 'Dear Leader,' is dead. He was found in his selfer, stabbed to death. The whereabouts of the self he was inhabiting at the time have not been reported at this time, but we are told that a suspect was caught in the act." The newscaster looked slightly off camera. "And this is incredible. I'm now being told that Gorn's internal camera had continued filming in the selfer, and we're getting footage of the alleged killer."

The screen cut to a close-up of a woman's face twisted in rage. She pulled back a little and her hand became visible, holding a laser knife and bringing it down repeatedly.

The officer gasped. "That's Grecia!"

"Who?" Lyndon asked.

"She's the one we all suspected went on Gorn's show—you know, Cat?"

The news program now showed a different shot of Grecia, wild-eyed and covered in blood, being led away from a building toward a vehicle in force-field cuffs. "Why'd you do it?" a journalist's voice called off-screen. The officers dragging her didn't stop, so she screamed back at the reporters as she was taken farther away.

"I wanted Halcyon to be better! I wanted to end the corruption, not destroy everything! That bastard deceived me! He used me!"

Lyndon and the two nuns stood in stunned silence as the news returned to the original correspondent repeating what had happened.

When the segment ended and an ad began, Lyndon turned it off. As if a spell had been broken, the three of them looked at the lifeless (and by now decidedly unlifelike) body of the man who had called himself Stark, then at one another with a dawning realization.

CHAPTER THIRTY-SIX

"You ready?" Lyndon asked Crenshaw. She closed her eyes for a second, then opened them, smiled, and nodded. They stepped onto the transport platform together. The attendant readied them for teleportation and began the computer-voiced countdown.

Seconds later they appeared in the Halcyon terminal. Lyndon stepped out first and held his hand out to Crenshaw, who rolled her eyes. "I'm not an invalid," she said, jumping lightly off the platform and breezing past him, out into the street. He shook his head with a little laugh and followed her.

"You don't feel weird at all, being back here?" he said.

"The only thing I still can't get used to is having you tagging along instead of a cameraman," she said haughtily, and hailed a driverless car.

It was a particularly beautiful day even for Halcyon. Exotic wildflowers nodded in a light breeze as the car whisked Crenshaw and Lyndon through the bright sunlight to the convent. The road had been extended and the last stop was now mere feet from a new door that had replaced the hidden entrance.

As they approached, a familiar-looking face appeared on a screen by the door, though Lyndon couldn't remember the name of the postulant. She recognized them before they could even say anything and broke into a grin. The door slid silently and smoothly into the side of the wall and the girl waved them in from an elevated perch next to it.

She wore neither the rough baggy dress that had been her uniform nor the flowing robes of a nun. Her clothing looked casual and contemporary. "Welcome!" she called, not waiting for permission to speak. Her tone had none of the fearful timidity uniformly exhibited by the postulants in the past, and Lyndon noticed her neck was bare. No tracker. "They're waiting for you in the office."

Lyndon grabbed Crenshaw's hand and she actually squeezed it back as they moved through the grounds. They were largely unchanged in appearance, yet somehow everything seemed brighter and livelier. Conversations and peals of laughter carried on the light breeze to their ears as all around them, women—and, Lyndon noted with surprise, what looked like a few men—went about their work and play.

They reached the building where the Mother Superior's office had been located and walked through the familiar hallway. The office door was wide open. Li and Crystal turned and smiled at them when they stepped in.

"Welcome back!" Crystal said. She ran the couple of steps toward them and embraced

Crenshaw tightly. Lyndon got a hug from her as well. He smiled back as they stepped back after the hug, still feeling apologetic over the way he had treated her, even though he no longer sensed any bitterness or resentment in her manner. She too wore regular street clothes—a bright patterned tunic over leggings.

"Thanks for inviting us," Crenshaw said. She and Lyndon took turns shaking Li's hand.

"Well, we wanted to show you what we've done with the place since your father's generous donation," Li said. "I'm sorry he couldn't make it. I hope he knows he's welcome here at any time."

"He sends his regrets," Crenshaw said. "Busy making deals, as always. He's going to try and meet us at the resort for dinner tonight." She laughed. "You're lucky he didn't come, actually—he'd be looking for a show idea or something." The others laughed too. "He's so grateful to you all for saving my life— twice! And he says to call on him any time you run into hardships again."

"Oh, the gift he gave us should keep us going for a long time," Li said. "Plus bookings are through the roof at the resort, thanks to good publicity from you two, and some more affordable packages we've started offering."

She led them out of the building and onto the grassy commons. "Besides, we've branched out—our members are pursuing arts and crafts, whatever they're interested in, and we plan to sell their work all over the galaxy."

"Members," Lyndon said. "That's a big change right there."

"Yes," Li said. "Although we still adhere to our religion and require all our members to do the same, we think of ourselves as a communal living organization rather than a religious order. There are levels of membership, but not like before." She nodded at Crystal. "This one co-chairs the advisory council with me. I can't imagine what I'd do without her." Crystal smiled, modest but confident.

"Lyndon!" a voice cried out from across the commons. A woman in a sundress made of a light, airy fabric flung herself into his arms before he could react. Her hair, considerably shorter than the last time he'd seen her, was a riot of shiny curls kept out of her eyes by a wide cloth headband. "I've been looking for you all day, hoping I'd run into you."

"Pella," Lyndon said with genuine affection, squeezing her soft curves in a tight hug and kissing her cheek. "It's so good to see you again; you look amazing."

"It's been a wild ride these past few months," Pella said, smiling. She patted her belly. "You can't tell yet, but I'm expecting a new member of the community in about seven months."

"Wow, congratulations!" Lyndon said, astonished.

"Yep," she said. "I can hardly believe it myself. That's the daddy over there!" She waved and a young man sitting in the grass with a group of men and women waved back from across the green, his broad smile visible even from a distance. Lyndon recognized the worker from the resort, although he'd changed the color of the streaks in his dreadlocks from silver to a warm yellow. "Quade was the first man to apply to join Halcyon after we voted to change our bylaws."

"Double congratulations, then," Lyndon said.

"Thanks!" Her relaxed, beaming face was a welcome sight to his eyes. "Well, we're in the middle of a seminar, so I have to get back. We'll see each other later, right?"

"Definitely," Lyndon said, also grinning happily by now.

She kissed his cheek once more and skipped back to her group. Li and Crystal continued the tour. They were taken to the food storage cave, which now had a teleporter installed. "Technology everywhere, eh?" Lyndon asked.

"Only where it really serves the mission of our community. We're adding it slowly and intentionally," Crystal explained. "We've started a food relief program, where we'll send Halcyon produce to parts of other planets where fresh food is scarce or nonexistent. Our first recipient, actually, is Mars. They're becoming a democratic society now that President Gorn's is gone—my goddess, was I ever brainwashed by that man!—but they lack basic resources after so many years of corruption. So we decided to help. There are so many good people on my home planet who deserve a chance at a better life."

She beamed. "Thanks to Mr. Connelly, we can now afford to do some good in the galaxy outside our own walls."

"You've changed just about everything since Deena left," Lyndon said.

"But it seems like you've gotten closer to the essence of your religion," Crenshaw put in. "'Life is precious.'"

"Yes," Crystal agreed, but her eyes were distant.

"How is she?" Lyndon asked, not sure what he wanted to hear.

"She's basically on house arrest on her own little plot of land," Li said, her face and voice neutral. "Twenty-four-hour video surveillance. She lives there alone, but some of the longer-standing members visit her from time to time."

Li saw the look on Crenshaw's face—even though she'd been given a say in the deal struck for Deena's cooperation, it had to be hard—and changed the subject. "I saw the news you caught the other killer," she said to Lyndon.

"We got his data from Gorn's selfer," he replied. "He used a self that looked like Lockwood Manette and a sensor jammer like Crenshaw's to get in and out of the convent." Gorn had been sure Crenshaw was planning to infiltrate the grounds, and he knew the scandal would be exponentially worse for Halcyon if the crime happened inside the convent, so he had the killer follow and attack her there.

They strolled toward the site of the pond while they talked. As they crested the gentle hill that led down toward it, Crenshaw slipped her hand into Lyndon's again. He gave it a squeeze and kept hold of it during their approach.

If they hadn't seen the pool of water with their own eyes before, they wouldn't have believed one had ever been there. A level field of rich soil and multicolored plants stood where the pond had been.

"We drained and permanently resealed the wellspring," Li said as they got closer. "We didn't want to hoard this gift for ourselves anymore, but we knew it wasn't possible to share it with the entire galaxy, so we gave it back to the planet." She tilted her head at Crenshaw. "You were the last person who'll ever be revived on Halcyon."

"Still, we're growing herbs on the site, and the medicines we make from them do a pretty remarkable job," Crystal put in. "I'm practically useless as a healer!"

"We won't be selling them commercially, but we'll give them to communities in need on other planets," Li continued. "And both of you and Mr. Connelly can have some whenever you need them."

"Plus, you're welcome to stay here instead of the resort, if you ever want an extra potent rejuvenation treatment," Crystal added. "The healing energies inside these walls are still way more powerful than at the spa."

"I can't believe you've done this much in six months!" Lyndon marveled.

Crystal nodded. "Once we started being able to voice our opinions and contribute ideas, it just sort of snowballed. Almost everyone agreed these changes were long overdue. And Mr. Connelly's gift made it possible to move fast."

They completed the tour of the grounds with a look at the far boundary, where the wall was being dismantled and expanded to accommodate more buildings. "We still want to grow very slowly so we stay tight-knit," Crystal said. "But we're accepting a few more applications now than we used to. And, of course, our members may choose to start families now, if they like." Lyndon smiled again, thinking of Pella's radiant face.

Before they left to meet Connelly, there was an informal gathering on the commons and a mildly intoxicating beverage flowed freely. Lyndon looked around in wonder at the change in atmosphere. It was as if the removal of the Mother Superior had released an ocean of bottled-up joy.

A tipsy Quade cornered Lyndon in the shade of a tree. "I want to thank you, man, for everything you did for Pella," he said. Lyndon looked to the side, quickly calculating whether he thought Pella would have told her partner everything.

Quade read his expression and smiled. "Yeah, even that," he said. Lyndon's face grew warm but he felt relieved. "She said the way you treated her with so much respect brought back her self-esteem, her sense of self, and that without it, she never would have gotten up the courage to ask me to join the community. So I need to thank you not only for her but for me. I knew I loved her the first time we ever met, but I never thought I could have this kind of happiness with her."

Lyndon felt embarrassed. "Really, I didn't do anything," he said.

Quade smiled, pleased. "See, man, you're just like she said. A lot of people would've taken advantage of that power and abused it.

Instead, you planted the seed in her mind that she deserved something better than what she was getting. She was actually thinking about leaving the order and seeing if I would come with her to start a new life, if Li hadn't changed everything when she did."

Quade shook his head wonderingly. "That would've been the best thing that ever happened to me in my whole life." He looked around at the happy throngs. "But this—this is even better." He turned back to Lyndon and enveloped him in a warm hug. Lyndon caught sight of Crenshaw over Quade's shoulder. He could tell she'd been looking at him but hastily pretended otherwise. Lyndon smiled to himself.

* * *

"So what's next for you, now that you're done with your victory tour of Halcyon?" Connor Connelly asked Lyndon teasingly. The glass walls of the private dining alcove atop one of Halcyon's restaurants gave them a view of trees below with countless twinkling lights in them. "Surely you're not going back to being a cop?"

"I don't know, sir," Lyndon said musingly. Connor had ordered and entreated him to call him by his first name, but he just couldn't break the habit. "I don't think I'll ever want to leave law enforcement, but—"

"But your career as an under-the-radar detective is kind of shot, unless you want to spend all your time in selfs," Crenshaw finished for him.

Lyndon laughed. "Pretty much," he said.

The overwhelming attention from the general public fascinated by his story only seemed to be increasing, and he didn't know if or when it would subside. He was mobbed wherever he went, and he'd gotten quickly used to seeing his face on screens everywhere.

"Commander Stoughton offered me a Chief of Police position, but I don't really want to supervise people and not be where the action is. At least not yet."

"What about you, daughter dear?" Connelly asked. "This is the longest you've been without a show; aren't you restless yet?"

"It still *feels* like I'm on a show," Crenshaw retorted. Requests for interviews and appearances with Lyndon had increased even from her formerly high-profile life.

Everyone knew what had happened on Halcyon—part of it anyway. Since they were helping conceal the convent's power of resurrection, the story was that she'd been in a coma and mistaken for dead when the nuns brought her back—but the public never seemed to tire of hearing it from Crenshaw's and Lyndon's own lips. "But yeah, I'm feeling ready to try something new soon."

"Well, I'll tell you one new thing you should try," Connelly said with an insinuating smile at Lyndon, who was by now accustomed enough to his flirtation not to flush red. "If you don't scoop him up soon, I don't know how much longer I can hold out myself."

"Oh my god, Dad," Crenshaw said in a tone of mock despair. "Will you give it a fucking rest?" But her foot in its high-heel shoe pressed lightly against Lyndon's boot. She didn't spare him a glance, but his body flooded with excitement. She apparently liked delaying what seemed inevitable, and truthfully he was enjoying the anticipation himself.

His sudden fame had brought countless adoring fans and he knew he had his pick of them, but he couldn't stop thinking about Crenshaw. The frequent close proximity due to their near-constant media appearances together didn't help.

"All right, I've got a real offer for you two," Connelly said. "I know you say you don't want to be a reality star anymore. But what if we combined your talents? A serious show starring both of you, going to distant worlds to investigate crimes? A different self every time? You'd be doing some real good in the galaxy, and I'd have a new hit on my hands."

Lyndon didn't think it was the worst idea; he'd quickly realized Crenshaw had more to offer than just being an adventure-seeking socialite. As soon as she'd gotten enough strength back after her second resurrection, she'd begun meddling in Lyndon and Li's plan to entrap the mysterious person who'd been harassing the Mother Superior.

They'd had plenty of blow-ups and struggles to gain the upper hand, but Crenshaw's innate sense of drama had helped immensely in planning Deena's approach. She'd insisted on the part where they offered everything but the convent grounds—convinced the person knew about the wellspring—and she'd been right.

The thought of more adventures with her quickened his heartbeat almost as much as her touch did.

Crenshaw raised her eyebrows and sipped her drink. "I'll have to think about it," she said to Connor. Her foot slipped out of her shoe and trailed lightly up Lyndon's leg. He did turn crimson this time. "I might try your other suggestion first."

ACKNOWLEDGMENTS

The patience and generosity of beta readers cannot be overstated. Jaclyn and Stevie, thank you for your time and attention, which helped *Eternal Order* be the best trashy retro nuns-in-space book it could be!